MO
BEHAVIOUR

I studied him further as he spoke. Eyes, deep set, dark and scarily sexy. Just the right amount of stubble on his chin. Razored hair that a fraction shorter or longer wouldn't have worked, but as it was worked to perfection. If I'd been hot after the dancing, I was even hotter now.

"You haven't told me your name."

I liked the way he said what he wanted to say, and with the minimum number of words.

"Chloe Dove," I said.

Look out for more brilliant reads from Point:

Kate Cann
Hard Cash
Shacked Up
Speeding
Footloose
Fiesta

Anne Cassidy
Tough Love
Missing Judy

Karen McCombie
My Funny Valentine
Blissed Out
Winter Wonderland
Love is the Drug
My Sister, the Superbitch

Louise Rennison
Angus, Thongs and Full-Frontal Snogging
It's OK, I'm Wearing Really Big Knickers
Knocked Out By My Nunga-Nungas

Catherine Robinson
Tin Grin
Celia

JUST DON'T LET YOUR LITTLE SISTER GET HER HANDS ON THEM...

MODEL
BEHAVIOUR

Geraldine Ryan

SCHOLASTIC

Scholastic Children's Books,
Commonwealth House, 1-19 New Oxford Street,
London, WC1A 1NU, UK
a division of Scholastic Ltd
London ~ New York ~ Toronto ~ Sydney ~ Auckland
Mexico City ~ New Delhi ~ Hong Kong

First published in the UK by Scholastic Ltd, 2002

ISBN 0 439 98130 1

Typeset by Falcon Oast Graphic Art Ltd
Printed by Cox and Wyman Ltd, Reading, Berks.

10 9 8 7 6 5 4 3 2 1

chapter one

It was the first day of the autumn half term and already I was looking for an excuse not to do my coursework. Enter Kelly Driscoll, my best friend, hammering on the front door fit to bust it.

"What you all dolled up for?" I wanted to know as she flounced into my room.

Kelly had a passion for Lycra and baby pink and on that particular day she had excelled herself. OK, so it was mild for the time of year, but this was dressing for clubbing not cramming, from her boob tube down to her strappy pink peep toe shoes – which for all their three-inch heels still failed to elevate her to the height of my shoulder. She reeked of CK One and was wearing so much lipgloss you could skate on it.

She batted her eyelids. I shivered in the draught. "Get your coat," she said. "We're going to the Fashion Show."

" 'Scuse me?" Sometimes with Kelly it was a good idea at least to attempt to put up a fight, just to show I had a mind of my own. I'd learned to do this not long after I met her when we were both in Year Seven at our old school. I'd been standing holding her Adidas bag waiting for her to come out of the loos and someone had bleated at me.

"How exactly d'you plan to smuggle us out of here?" I demanded, like a character in a prison escape B-movie. If she'd suggested digging a tunnel and produced a spade from somewhere I wouldn't have been in the least surprised.

She gave me a pitying look. "It's half term, Chloe! What's the big deal?"

"It's all right for you," I said. "Try telling my mother that."

For Kelly, college was just a laugh. It meant that if she chose the right subjects she could do all her favourite things: watch telly (Media Studies), see a few films (Film Studies) and show off in front of an audience (Drama) — something she'd been doing all her life anyway. She'd got some idea about applying to uni to do Performing Arts, but if it didn't work out then there was always a place for her in her dad's business. She was bound to be discovered sooner or later, anyway, as she was fond of reminding me.

Both my parents were teachers and education was a priority in our household, which meant I was trapped on the merry-go-round of Further Education until I'd got my A levels. Then, whoopee! I'd really get lucky. The thrilling prospect of university meant I'd be allowed to do another three years' worth of exams. Wasn't life wonderful!

"Leave your mum to me," Kelly said, not in the least bit fazed. Well, she wouldn't be. She'd not endured the half-hour lecture on the perils of leaving everything to the last minute.

I trailed after her into the kitchen where Mum, sitting at the table, was flicking through Delia's *How To Cook*. Not that it would make any difference. She still wouldn't be able to.

"I've got this essay all about costume, Mrs Dove, only I'm not sure where to start. Chloe's so good at dates and words and stuff," Kelly pleaded with her.

Mum, amazingly, bought it. I think she saw Kelly as someone who needed moral guidance – not being in the same fortunate position as myself, blessed with parents for whom education was so much more important than material possessions. Ha, ha.

I struggled into my jacket, just a tad annoyed for being such a wimp and allowing Kelly to rescue me, like I was Rapunzel unable to come up with a means of escape on my own. But that was the difference between Kelly and me. Where I saw problems, Kelly saw only opportunity.

Checking my appearance I couldn't help noticing that there was orange juice on my T-shirt, and my hair was a mess, but Kelly insisted it would only arouse Mum's suspicions if I spent ages getting dolled up, and anyway we were running short of time. The Fashion Show started prompt at two, she said, and we'd never get to the front of the crowd if we didn't leave immediately.

It occurred to me to make some comment about the length of time she had spent titivating herself, and wouldn't it have been nice if she'd given me just a bit more warning before she landed on me so

I could have been doing likewise – but I didn't bother. She'd got me out of the house, at least. Besides, I reasoned, as I grabbed my sister's bike from the garage (mine had a puncture I couldn't afford to get repaired), what was the point of getting tarted up when there were going to be proper models around? Who would notice me among that lot?

chapter two

We parked our bikes outside Superdrug with the one lock we had between us. Kelly wanted to nip inside to top up her perfume before we headed for the Mall, but I persuaded her that as far as CK One was concerned, less was definitely more. Besides, we were late. From the mix of pulsating dance music and the ghetto drawl of the MC above it, the entertainment was well under way.

The Mall was heaving, and the area round the raised catwalk was six deep in excited spectators all waiting restlessly for the models to come on. I pulled my jacket tighter around me, cursing the fact that oranges contained so much juice, and legged it after Kelly.

"Hurry up, Chloe," she yelled at me, pink with anticipation. "Use your elbows."

It was a joke with Kelly — although not one I appreciated — that my elbows were my best feature. Like the rest of me they are angular. Over the years, my elbows — with the help of my stonking big feet — had delivered us safely to the front of the crowd at many a gig. Great for us, not so great for any person of normal height trying to see over my six-foot-with-heels frame.

Finally, we were where we wanted to be. You would have had to be dead — or my dad — not to be whipped along by the mood of anticipation that rippled through the waiting crowd. Whenever I hear music something switches on inside me like a light, and the louder the music the stronger my compulsion to move my body becomes.

Kelly was pretending to be completely unfazed by the music and the lights and the sheer hype of it all, though she must have been as excited as I was, if you considered how long she'd spent tarting herself up. After about five more minutes the music faded and the MC stepped forward.

"OK everybody," he drawled. "Give it up now for the models of the Olympus Model Agency."

The crowd duly cheered. Kelly whipped out a mirror to check her face.

"And remember," he continued. "While you-all is lookin' up at dem-all, model scouts Angie, Ray and Tina will be in da house. Tink about it, it could be YOU up here next year, alongside dese quality chicks and geezers."

A deafening roar went up at these words and you could have had your eye poked out by all the combs and mascara wands that appeared as if from nowhere. The predominantly female audience was by this time approaching hysteria.

Kelly turned round to me and winked. "Was I right to wear this outfit or was I right?" she yelled over the noise. "Bet you I get signed up!" She reapplied her lipgloss and gave me a sweet smile. Remembering my orange-stained T-shirt I could have kicked her. But I forgot about it as soon as the lighting changed and the pounding music started up again. At last, the show was under way.

It was great! Not so much the clothes – which came from the usual chain stores you see on every high street – but the models! I'd never seen such stunning specimens in all my life. Girls and boys of every ethnic origin burst on to the catwalk in pairs or singly, swaying to the music and taking over the space like it was their God-given right. Confidence oozed out of every pore. In as far as they each possessed two arms, two legs and a head, they looked like the rest of us, but there the resemblance ended – it was as if they were from a parallel planet where all imperfections had been airbrushed away.

It was the arrogant stance that singled them out from the crowd who gawped up at them from below, their sheer in-your-face look-at-me-if-you-dare haughtiness. I stared, open-mouthed, as they wove in and out in a brilliantly choreographed display of athleticism, just missing colliding at each turn, never looking anywhere but straight ahead, and each wearing expressions of supremely studied indifference.

I was in my element. The group of spectators we found ourselves squashed in amongst were all swaying and clapping in time to the music, arms waving in the air, and I couldn't help join in. Occasionally I gave Kelly a sidelong look. She was doing her best to appear ultra-cool – just in case one of the scouts was looking her way, probably. I decided to leave her to it and concentrated instead on having a good time.

All too soon it was over, and the MC was back on the stage thanking us for being such a great audience. Kelly and I fell on one another with excited shrieks. Arm in arm we jostled our way through the throng that was beginning to disperse now, swapping opinions on what we'd seen. Kelly, of course, had fallen in love with at least two of the male models.

"How can I look at ordinary college boys again after I've witnessed those guys!" she exclaimed.

"Would you really want a boyfriend who was better-looking than you were?" I taunted. "You wouldn't be able to stand the competition. Besides, you'd never be able to keep up on your little legs."

Still hyper, I adapted my walk to a hip-swivelling sashay, then held the pose, while Kelly applauded sarcastically. "I'm not sure about the T-shirt, though," she said. "Orange juice is so-o last season. Now, are you going to unlock these bikes, or do we have to stand here freezing our butts off for the rest of the afternoon?"

Suddenly I felt desperately flat. The fun was over. There was nothing to look forward to but an evening in my room planning my Hamlet essay, followed by four more days of the same. It was as I was bending to unlock the bikes and thinking how sad I must be if the highlight of my week was ER and the Hollyoaks omnibus, that I felt a hand on my shoulder.

chapter three

"I've been following you two ever since you left the show."

Such distinctly dodgy words would normally have put me on my guard immediately. However, I felt far less threatened when I eventually struggled to my feet and registered the skinny little guy, dressed in black leather from top to toe, standing in front of me. His eyes barely drew level with my chest, for a start, so unless he was carrying a knife I gave myself a pretty good chance of being able to defend myself should he decide to start any funny business.

"Are we doing anything illegal?" I asked, although he didn't look like a security guard.

Normally, Kelly, always up for a ruck, would

have attacked at the first provocation, but oddly she seemed struck dumb. She gazed at the man's chest, transfixed, and she'd gone pink in the face. She'd obviously noticed something about this munchkin that I'd failed to spot from my crouching position up against the back wheels of our bikes, where I'd been struggling to remove her pedal from the spokes of my wheel, so she didn't have to get oil on her best clothes.

She suddenly started sending out pulling signals as if it were Tom Cruise standing there. Was I missing something or what? Fair enough, he was the right height for Tom, but there the resemblance ended. This guy had way too much jaw and his lips were practically invisible they were so thin. He had one of those little sculpted beards and greasy black hair that hung limply over one narrow eye.

When he flashed a smile his teeth sparkled. Not like in the Colgate advert, but because he had a chip of diamond in one of his front teeth. A smile was supposed to light up your face, but all it did for this guy was to make him look even more sinister, if that were possible. Kelly tossed her blonde mane madly and dimpled up for him, but whatever he had was lost on me.

"You guys were at the show, right?" he drawled, in that lazy public-school kind of way you didn't get to hear much round these parts. "Tell me what you thought of it."

Kelly began to enthuse, imitating his accent and pulling out all the stops. Odd, though, that even while she was going on and on about how wonderful everything had been, the Oompa Loompa was clearly impatient for her to shut up. But Kelly, well into her stride now, was oblivious. It was all getting a bit embarrassing, but without actually telling her to shut up before she made an even bigger fool of herself I couldn't think of a way of helping her out.

Tom Thumb finally cut her off mid-flow, turned to me and drawled: "I was watching you dance. You really seemed to be getting into it."

"Me?" I squeaked.

He volunteered another brief flash of his creepy smile. I liked him better mean. Then he said: "Have you ever thought about modelling?"

Kelly burst into unrestrained peals of laughter. "What, like before and after photos?" she said.

"I wasn't talking to you, actually."

Kelly's jaw dropped. Who did this guy think he was?

14

As if he'd read my mind he began to introduce himself. At the exact moment he gave his name I spotted the badge on his lapel which read *Ray Malone, Official Scout for Olympus Model Agency.* There was a London telephone number below.

"What's your name, kid?" he asked me.

I stammered it out. "Chloe Dove," I said.

He nodded thoughtfully. "I'd have said you stood five ten, right?" he asked me.

I nodded, something like hysteria bubbling up in my chest. This whole situation was just surreal. I stared, fascinated, as he poked about inside his ear with his little finger then inspected what was on the end of it. Kelly, an only child and a bit more particular than most about that sort of thing, flared her nostrils and grimaced.

"How do we know you're not pulling a stunt?" she asked him. I was grateful to her for voicing an obvious question, because I'd suddenly turned into a complete idiot and needed all the help I could get.

"If you have any doubts that I am who I say I am, my lovely, then I suggest you ring this number and ask Serena Montague, who runs Olympus, to verify that I'm one of her scouts. I think you'll find she says yes."

His tone, like his front tooth, would have cut glass. It was hard to know what must have been making Kelly fume more – being called "my lovely" or not being the centre of Ray Malone's attention. Once more he fixed me with his manic stare.

"You still haven't answered my question, Chloe Dove," he said. "I asked if you'd ever thought about modelling."

Kelly, even more put out now, had clearly decided on an alternative strategy. If Ray Malone was not going to fall for her charms then she would withdraw from the conversation. Cool as you like, she removed her phone from her bag and began to check her messages. You had to admire her nerve.

"I – I don't know," I stuttered. "I've never thought I was the type. I don't look like a model."

"Believe me, you are very much the type." He handed me a card. "I want you to go home and have a chat with your mum and dad. Get them to call me, or do it yourself. Then we'll arrange a proper meeting."

Dumbly, I took the card from him and slid it into my back pocket, unread.

"Be seeing you," he said, and flashed his jewelled

tooth at me again. I watched him walk away with the stride of a man whose legs were twice as long, until he merged in with the shoppers heading home.

"Well," Kelly fumed. "What a horrible little man. I hope you're not seriously going to consider his offer."

I fingered the card in my jeans pocket and wondered what my mum and dad would do with this piece of news.

"Dunno," I said, trying to make light of the encounter.

"'Spect when you ring up you'll find out he's just some jumped-up office boy who gets off trying to pull ridiculously tall girls," she snapped.

I chose to ignore the words "ridiculously tall". Instead, determined to keep the peace, I humoured Kelly by slagging off her new worst enemy.

"Maybe you're right. Munchkin or what?" I said, which raised a smile.

For all I knew, Kelly might have been right about Ray Malone's motives. What was so special about me, after all? Particularly when you put me next to her. She was the one who stood out in a crowd, with her gorgeous figure and the bouncy personality that seemed to attract boys like bubblegum to the sole of a shoe.

I tried to talk about something else for the rest of the way home, but nothing I said made any difference to Kelly's bad mood. Kelly's silences could speak volumes and pretty soon I was doing everything I could to convince her – and myself, naturally – that there'd obviously been some mistake.

My explanation went like this. Ray Malone had been told to find some tall girls for some weird Benetton advert or something. If I was foolish enough to take up his offer and go round to this Olympus Agency, wherever it was, I'd find myself in a line-up with hundreds of others. Then after five minutes I'd be out on my ear. They needed me to make up the numbers, that was all. It seemed to satisfy Kelly, and by the time we parted ways her good humour was almost fully restored.

chapter four

Lindsay started on me as soon as I got through the back door. She was hacking her way through a large white loaf and believe me, from the murderous look she gave me, I was convinced I was next.

"Who said you could borrow my bike?" she yelled. "You know I've got my paper round to do. I had to walk it all that way."

Although Lindsay barely reached my shoulder, she was so full of righteous anger that I shrank in her presence. Besides, as I said, she had a knife. In the circumstances I thought it best if I apologized with all the sincerity I could muster. I clapped my hand over my mouth.

"Oh, Lindsay," I said. "I completely forgot about your paper round."

Actually, I hadn't so much forgotten about it as done my usual trick of completely dismissing the fact that I even had a sister. I'd been desperate to get out of the house. My bike had a puncture and I needed transport. There was a spare bike in the garage. I took it. End of story. Only it was becoming apparent that there was a second instalment.

Mum came bustling into the kitchen then, complete with wooden spoon, to stir up more trouble.

"You know, Chloe," she began. "It's about time you started taking other people's feelings into consideration a bit more. Lindsay's had to haul that big heavy bag full of papers all round the estate, you know."

She stuck the spoon in the pot that was bubbling on the cooker hob, licked it, pulled a face and sprinkled in some salt.

"Do her good," I muttered. "Might get rid of some of that puppy fat."

Lindsay was slapping enough peanut butter on her bread to paste a roll of wallpaper with. "I'm not fat," she wailed. "Mum, will you tell her. Just 'cos she looks like a beanpole she thinks anyone who's got curves is abnormal."

My insult had been a half-hearted one. But I was

feeling peeved that so far no one had given me the opportunity to make my announcement. Then I remembered that according to what my mum thought, I'd been in the library all afternoon. Shit! There was nothing for it but to keep on bickering with Lindsay in order to keep Mum's mind off the subject of my still undone coursework.

"Beanpole," I sneered. "Now there's an original insult."

I stared at Lindsay hard, perhaps for the first time in ages. Actually, she was right. She wasn't fat — exactly. But overnight, it seemed to me, her shape had changed. Only yesterday she'd been a little girl with stumpy legs and a flat chest. Now she had the full complement — boobs, bum, hips and thighs. Some might say she was shapely, others — like that Ray Malone from the model agency — might not be so kind. It was completely extraordinary how I'd managed to miss my kid sister's evolution from child to woman.

Maybe she was getting her periods, too. She was nearly thirteen, after all. For all I knew she'd been getting them for months, but Lindsay and I had never gone in for exchanging confidences. Perhaps our lack of closeness was due to the five-year gap.

After all, I still remember Mum breastfeeding her and changing her disgusting nappies! It would have taken a huge leap of faith for me to start thinking of her as a human being.

Lindsay was still waiting for Mum to take her side. "No, of course you're not fat, sweetheart," she clucked. Then, in the next breath, she added: "But you soon will be if you carry on eating between meals like that."

I stuck out my tongue in victory. Lindsay returned the gesture. Fortunately, Mum had turned her back. "We'll be having supper in an hour's time, so why you need to be making peanut-butter sandwiches now I don't know. Anyway, did you manage to get Kelly's research done? Although why you let her boss you around like that when you've got your own work to do I'll never understand."

I decided to humour her. "I was just about to put in some work on my Hamlet before supper, actually," I lied.

"It's your turn to set the table," Lindsay yelled after me as I made my escape.

That was one good thing about doing A levels, I decided as I lay on my bed. No one expected you to do as many chores when you were pleading deadlines. Of course, it was another reason why Lindsay hated me, but I could live with that. Right now, I had to work out my story for the dinner table.

Although as it turned out, it couldn't have been easier.

"Ruby Houlder wanted me to go down the Burleigh Centre this afternoon to watch that Fashion Show. Only I couldn't get there because I had no bike." Lindsay gave me a meaningful glare and reached across me for the pitta bread.

"Manners," I said. "Would you like a pitta, Dad?" I held out the basket like a model child. Unfortunately, Dad didn't notice how polite I was being on account of never noticing anything much. The only way I was going to prevent Lindsay from getting back to the subject of bikes, I realized, was to drop my own bombshell.

"Oh, the fashion show," I said, nonchalantly. "Actually, Kelly and me managed to see a little bit of that on our way back from the library."

"Surprise, surprise," Mum said. She was obviously too weary now to pursue the conundrum of how Kelly and I had managed to find ourselves in the Burleigh Centre on our way back from the library when the two were at opposite ends of the town.

"Actually something rather strange happened to me while I was down there," I continued.

Mum and Lindsay's identical brown eyes were on my face. Lindsay had even stopped chewing. Not Dad, though. I waited for him to acknowledge me, which he finally did, albeit grudgingly, and then I told them.

Lindsay, predictably, started on the wisecracks. "You mean you were with Kelly and they said they wanted you to ring them up and arrange a meeting?" she sneered. "What exactly are you going to be modelling for? *The Big Issue?*"

"Oh, very funny," I said. I pulled out the card Ray Malone had given me, and tossed it on to the table where it narrowly missed landing in Mum's wine glass. So far she'd said nothing – which was a surprise. Neither had Dad – which was par for the course. She picked up the card. Flicking a grain of rice off it, she began to read out the information.

"And what does Miss Driscoll think about this?" Mum asked.

"She's cool about it," I said, defensively.

Mum gave a wry smile. "I bet," she said. "I still remember her face that time when you were both in the juniors and you won the dancing competition."

"For God's sake, that was years ago," I said. "She's not like that any more. I told you, she's cool about it."

Mum didn't look convinced, but she let it drop and handed the card to Dad who read it about fifty times. Dad is suspicious by nature. I can imagine him as a little boy at Christmas on Santa's lap, demanding to know the catch.

"You're not to follow this up, Chloe," he said. "Anyone can have a card printed out these days. This bloke could be a pimp, for all we know."

"What's a pimp, Dad?" Lindsay asked innocently, only not so innocently.

Dad glared at her. I explained to him, as patiently as I could, that the name of this man had been announced from the catwalk and besides, he was wearing an official badge with his photograph on it.

"He even insisted one of you phone the agency to check it out," I added, for good measure.

"You can't argue with that, Tony," Mum said.

I made a silent promise to be kinder to her.

It was clear from the desperate look on Dad's face that he was casting about for another straw. I knew him well enough to guess what it would be and hey, ho, correcto.

"What about your A levels? It's hardly the moment to start taking on something like this with everything you've got in front of you," he said. He looked at Mum for support, but she seemed intent on her plate.

"You don't seem to mind me slaving away at the sandwich shop every Saturday for a pittance," I said.

Touché, without a doubt. That sandwich shop job was the bane of my life. I sometimes thought that if I had to spend another Saturday morning mixing tuna mayonnaise I would lob it from the back of a spoon at the next customer who walked in.

My logic was irrefutable when I added: "If I got modelling work I could pick and choose when I wanted to do it, for a start, and because it's proper money I wouldn't have to do it so often, would I?"

Was he happy with that?

What do you think?

"Money's not everything, Chloe," he said.

"Oh, is that right?" I asked him. I was getting seriously pissed off now. Why could no one be happy for me? I could imagine Kelly's mum jumping a metre in the air if Kelly had been given this opportunity. My parents only ever showed pride in me if I got a good school report.

"So money's not everything, is it? Well, it seems to be everything to me. Isn't that why I'm going to university, so I can make more money than I would if I left school at eighteen? After I've paid back my loan, that is. You never know, I might end up having a fabulous teaching job like you. Then I'll be able to afford to run an eight-year-old car and never spend a holiday abroad unless it's in a tent, self-catering."

Dad was a lecturer at a further education college. As he was fond of telling us, he made loads less than a teacher in an ordinary school would and he didn't get their holidays either.

Mum spoke up at last. "Don't talk to your father like that," she said. "He works very hard to support you girls. We both do. It'd be nice to be appreciated for once."

"I appreciate you," Lindsay piped up smugly.

I had a strong desire to stick her head in the remains of the chilli. This conversation was not heading in the direction I'd planned. Instead of being the recipient of an outpouring of family pride, I was the villain of the piece. I decided to change tack and went all wounded martyr on them. Well, it worked for Lindsay often enough.

"I thought you'd be pleased for me," I said. "I thought you'd all fall over the idea of me bringing a bit of money into the house so you won't need to bankrupt yourselves when I go to university. If I ever get an offer, that is. I suppose I'll just throw this card in the bin. It'll all probably come to nothing anyway. Nothing exciting ever happens to me."

Leaden-faced, I turned my attention to a clump of congealed rice on my plate. When Lindsay said that it was obvious the scout had meant to give the card to Kelly anyway, Mum told her to shut up, which was some comfort at least. We carried on eating, each immersed in our own thoughts, until Mum suddenly spoke up.

"You know, it can't do any harm just to give them a ring, Tony," she said.

chapter five

But for all sorts of reasons I didn't. I spent the rest of the week between drafting my Shakespeare essay, bickering with Lindsay and mulling things over. A lot of time was spent studying myself in the brown-speckled full-length mirror in my bedroom and wondering what exactly Ray Malone had seen when he'd said with such conviction that I was modelling material. Until now, I'd always thought my face was nondescript, like a blank canvas. Look at me and you'd have no idea what I was thinking. I'd gone through school being accused of looking bored by teachers even when actually I'd been enjoying the lesson.

What about the rest of me? Well, I suppose I've

got good teeth. Eighteen years and no fillings. I don't have spots or freckles or hairy warts. Both my eyebrows and my cheekbones have been singled out as my best features by my mother. Scratching around for compliments, or what? As for the rest of me, it goes something like this — hair: mousy, if you're being cruel, otherwise light brown; eyes: blue-grey; mouth: large (no getting away from it); nose: definitely too big, my father's nose, and as different from my mum's and Lindsay's little blobs as you can imagine.

I've inherited his height and skinniness too. Trousers or shirts off the peg never fitted because the arms and legs are always far too short, which meant I'd spent most of my life in jeans and T-shirts. While Kelly was a perfect ten, five five and looked right in everything she put on — if slightly overdressed for my taste. Not that I was jealous or anything. *Moi?*

The rest of the week dragged by with me dithering about what to do and being just as far from making up my mind at the end of the week as I'd been at the beginning of it. I got as far as dialling the first four digits three or four times but always my nerve went at the last minute and I ended up slamming the phone down. *OK, I wasn't proud of myself!*

Funnily enough, considering how much she'd sulked about it, it was Kelly who finally helped me decide what to do. I hadn't seen her since the day of the Fashion Show, since she'd spent the rest of the week – when I'd been holed up with my books – running round the country visiting various doting relatives and no doubt being showered with money and presents at every stop-off point. But she was waiting for me outside the school gates on that first morning.

"Any news?" she demanded, clearly desperate to catch the next instalment, but pretending not to be.

I did my best to appear nonchalant. "Well, I managed to get my Hamlet essay out of the way," I said.

She scowled at me. "For God's sake, Chloe. As if I'm interested in that! I mean have you phoned the agency yet?"

"Oh, that," I said, trying to sound as indifferent as I could.

The worst thing you could do with Kelly was to show her that you wanted something. I hadn't thought of that dance competition that Mum had brought up round the supper table the other night for years, but it was a good example. I'd won it fairly and squarely, but Kelly wouldn't accept the result. She swore I'd won because the judges didn't like the music she'd chosen and because her costume was a proper one from a real theatrical costumier and they'd been told to pick the girl who looked as if her costume had been home-made.

The feeling had been creeping up on me all week that here was something that, actually, I wouldn't mind having – a rare enough event. OK, so Kelly wasn't in any position to compete with me over it, but already she was beginning to belittle my achievement. It wouldn't be long, I was pretty sure, before she came up with some notion that model agencies were two a dime and the only one anybody thought was any good was Storm.

"I knew you wouldn't ring," she said. "Honestly, Chloe, you can be such a wimp at times. Still, it's probably for the best, my mum says."

"Why's that then?" It hadn't escaped my notice that Kelly seemed positively relieved I hadn't followed things up.

"Well, like I said. It could be a hoax. What if you

put yourself through the humiliation of asking for Ray Malone and they've never heard of him? Or worse. What if it wasn't a hoax, but when you turned up they decided you weren't what they were looking for. Just think how disappointed you'd be then."

From where I was standing it looked like Chloe and her mum had spent the best part of the week discussing my predicament. I felt a twitch of irritation.

"I haven't said I'm not going to phone them *at all*, have I? Just that I haven't done it yet. I'm just considering my options," I said, not having a clue what this meant but thinking it sounded rather grand.

"Options? Like what options?"

I shrugged. "You know, how I'm going to fit it in with college work. When I can give my notice in at the sandwich shop. That sort of thing," I said.

Kelly tried another tactic. The one that went, if you don't want to hear something, ignore it. "Shit!" she squeaked. "Is that the time? I said I'd meet someone in the canteen before registration."

It was a rare thing for me ever to come to an important decision. Normally I kind of just let decisions make themselves, which might have been why so far in my life I'd never felt in control of events. But as I strolled into college on that grey and windy Monday morning I knew that, finally, I was on the way to taking my life firmly into my own hands. This time I wasn't going to wimp out. I was going to make that call to the agency as soon as I got home.

chapter six

In a bid to keep our phone bill in single figures, my thrifty father had installed our phone in the kitchen. This certainly had the desired effect. The through traffic in our kitchen made the M11 look like a shanty road, and I'd lost count of the number of times I'd been forced to slam down the receiver on Kelly, just as I'd started telling her a particularly juicy bit of gossip, because someone had wandered in looking for something! In order to have any privacy at all in our house you had to wait until the house was empty. It rarely was after four-thirty, and the only reason it happened to be now was that Lindsay was doing her paper round and Mum and Dad were both at meetings.

Clumsily, with one ear cocked for the sound of the car drawing up, and one eye on the back door through which Lindsay's fluorescent newspaper sack – with her close behind – might appear at any second, I picked out the numbers. Within moments, the ringing tone came through. I felt sick with nerves, but gritted my teeth, determined to stick with it after my conversation with Kelly earlier. A message box clicked on and Ray Malone was suddenly introducing himself.

As calmly as I could I left my name and phone number and a cursory "Please ring back." Then, my heart still working overtime, I replaced the receiver with a shaky hand and retreated to my room.

Since the Fashion Show, I'd taken to flicking through the glossy magazines whenever I popped into the newsagent's for my daily supply of Wrigley's Extra. At first glance many of the girls on the pages of the fashion spreads looked nothing like as pretty as some of the girls I went to college with. Kelly, for one, I thought, would have wiped the floor with most of them. But they were all, without exception, stick thin, with long legs and arms and bodies that showed off the clothes they wore to perfection. They all had their own strong individual look – but in common they exhibited the sleek and cosseted sheen of pedigree cats. What struck me most about them, though, was how far removed from ordinary life they all appeared.

My room was too small to attempt the runway walk I'd observed at the Fashion Show, but now I started to have a go at imitating some of the poses. After a few tries I began to flatter myself that my attempts were almost passable, so I sat on my bed and began to work on some facial expressions. I did sultry, coy, and I was just going for urban cowgirl when I heard the phone. I was out of my room like a rat from a trap, but Lindsay, who must have let herself in through the back door at just the moment the phone sprang into life, got there first.

"Some male," she said, disdainfully, and held the phone out.

I pressed the receiver nervously to my ear. It was him. Ray Malone.

"Chloe? Good to hear from you. Have you spoken to your parents yet?"

"Er, yes."

"Good. Well that's a start. What do they think?"

"How long have you got?"

Ray Malone apparently found my remark quite amusing. After he'd stopped hooting he asked me when I'd be free to go down to London to meet Serena.

I was numb with a mixture of fear and excitement. *It's going to happen*, I kept saying to myself. *It's really going to happen. I didn't dream it after all.*

"I can come next Wednesday afternoon," I said. Wednesdays were supposed to be for physical recreation but I can't say I'd ever taken up the opportunity. I could take Kelly along.

"Excellent. Get here for three. I'll send you directions. You'll have your mum with you, won't you? Just in case you were thinking of bringing a friend. Mums are much more sensible."

"Oh, right." So, Kelly would be spending Wednesday afternoon skiving on her own then.

"Just remember. No make-up and wear your hair loose. We're going to be taking some polaroids, so you'll need a change of clothes too. Skirt, trousers, couple of different tops. Don't go out and buy anything, though. It's you we want to see, not your wardrobe."

"Oh, don't worry," I said. "That's not worth a second glance."

He hooted again, said goodbye and put the phone down. At some stage in the conversation, Mum and Dad must have come in. When I looked round, there they were, hovering, still in their outdoor coats. Lindsay was trying to attract Mum's attention but Mum swatted her away, irritably, clearly desperate for me to relate the conversation I'd just had.

"Just wait a bit, Linds, for goodness' sake," she said. "Don't you want to know what Chloe and that agency man have been talking about?"

"Not really," Lindsay said, "but I expect she's going to tell us. It's just that I don't want chips again. We always have chips on Monday."

"Oh, shut up, do," Mum said. "Now go on, Chloe."

I repeated the conversation, almost word for word, while Mum and Dad listened, Mum's mouth practically dropping open with excitement and Dad's face growing increasingly suspicious. Lindsay, meanwhile, was rummaging in the freezer for an alternative to a) oven chips and b) me being the centre of attention.

"Get the chips out, Lindsay," Mum said. "I'll do us some beans and a fried egg each, too." She looked flustered.

"By rights we should be having champagne to celebrate," I said, finally daring to believe that next Wednesday I was going to London to be signed up as a model.

"Why didn't we get a bottle of wine on the way home? I said we should, didn't I, Tony? Only you said we'd only drink it if we got one."

My dad's logic was flawless. "Perhaps we should leave the celebrations till we see a contract," he said. "There's many a slip 'twixt cup and lip."

"Who wants what then?" Mum asked. "Chloe?"

"Everything, please, Mum. I'm starving," I said.

"You'll have to start watching what you eat now you're a model," said Dad.

"Not her," Mum said. "She's got your genes to be grateful to for her figure." Mum wasn't complimenting me as much as being nice to Dad for not making a scene. It seemed he'd finally come round. We could all relax at last. Or so I thought.

"Lindsay? Chips, egg and beans?"

Lindsay scowled at Mum. "I said I didn't want chips again, didn't I? Why does no one ever listen to me?"

Then she stomped out of the kitchen and headed for her room.

"Touch of the green-eyed monster, what do you think, Tony?" Mum arranged the chips, like lifeless fingers, on two baking trays.

"Well, we can't all be models." From his face it was clear that he was baffled why anyone would want to be. "Do her a few chips. She'll come down when she smells them."

We all had a bit of a giggle.

chapter seven

The following Wednesday we caught the midday train to King's Cross. We'd bought baguettes from the station café, but I felt so sick with nerves that I couldn't eat any of mine at all.

Mum must have picked this up because she leaned across and patted my hand. "You know, this isn't an examination, Chloe," she said. "You've passed that. Remember, they've already decided they like you, otherwise they wouldn't be wasting their time seeing you."

I hadn't thought of that.

"Just think about all those girls sending their photos to model agencies week after week and never hearing anything. You've jumped that hurdle already. You're way ahead of most of the competition, if you think about it."

I hadn't thought of that either. Relief flooded in and by the time the train drew into the station, I'd quite cheered up.

We found the agency easily. Blake House turned out to be a disappointingly characterless high-rise building down a seedy side street cluttered with overflowing bins. We went in through the revolving doors to the lobby and came face to face with a man in a navy uniform who looked like some sleazy extra from *The Bill*. Pointing to the lift he muttered, "Forflor." *So far, so ordinary*, I thought.

But once the lift opened on to the fourth floor, we were catapulted into a very different world indeed. The reception area was more like an art gallery than anything else. The stark white walls were mounted with huge black and white photos of the models who presumably worked for the agency, as well as framed certificates declaring that the Olympus Agency was a member of AMA, whatever that was. A couple of elegant white leather settees had been tastefully arranged around a circular glass coffee table which was strewn with the latest editions of the fashion monthlies.

Against one wall, a huge marble aquarium caught my eye. Fish, all dazzlingly different colours, shapes and sizes, swam around, dodging and weaving in out of each other just like the models I'd seen on the catwalk the day Ray Malone had walked into my life. Salsa music played low and a light, fresh citrus scent overlaid the whole room.

The receptionist continued to speak in guarded tones to whoever it was at the other end of her phone. I wasn't expecting the enthusiastic welcome she gave us when finally she put it down.

"So sorry," she said. "Unsolicited." She pulled a face.

I managed to stammer out my name, wondering what on earth she was talking about.

"Hi-i, Chloe! Ooh! So you're here! Let me just give Serena a call."

Her manicured fingers tapped out a number and then she purred:

"We've all been dy-ing to meet you, you know. I'm Camilla, by the way."

I looked at the floor, terrified. If this was the effect the receptionist had on me, how on earth would I cope with the big guns? Fortunately, before I had time to work this one out, the big guns were out and pointing my way. I never thought I'd be so relieved to see Ray Malone, but at least he was a familiar face. He flashed his spooky diamond smile at me.

Serena Montague was far more intimidating than Ray Malone, but in a very different way. She was tall, willowy and dressed in a floaty white outfit that gave her the appearance of a film star dropping in to collect her Oscar.

"Oh, Ray, darling," she breathed, huskily. "I do believe you've gone and done it again."

She took hold of my shoulders and some awkward air-kissing went on, with me not having a clue how to do it, as usual. It was a huge relief that she didn't try this with Mum because I am convinced that if she had, Mum would have dropped everything and fled. Instead, she held out an elegant hand and shook my mother's firmly. I noticed Mum's jaw was set in the same rictus grin mine was. Thoughts of Yorick's skull danced through my brain and for a brief moment I wanted to be back in the classroom, half asleep, while Miss Frazer droned on about symbolism.

"Think you can do anything with her, Charlie?"

I was beginning to register the rest of the group,

now. Charlie was clearly the photographer, from the way he walked round me and eyed me up and down from all angles. He was my height, with a tangle of grey hair and a paunch that was as out of place in this environment as a cleavage in a nunnery.

"Reckon I could have a go."

Ray Malone looked on, rubbing his jaw between finger and thumb, as if asking himself exactly why he'd thought I'd ever had any potential, which was hardly conducive to building up my confidence. There was someone else there too, but I was too scared to move my head and see what other monster lurked in the wings. I was beginning to feel like a prize cow, I can tell you.

Serena Montague clapped her hands and said: "Chloe, Mrs Dove, coffee in my room. Charlie, you come too. See you later, Ray, darling."

Then it was about turn and down a corridor, white of course, more black and white pictures of models staring at me from the walls, more greenery and yards more pristine carpet. Finally we were in Serena's room. She ushered us into low chairs, then elegantly poured coffee into white china cups. That done, Serena draped herself gracefully against her desk which held only a tele-phone, a laptop and a thick black file edged in gold. Charlie lurked in a corner, seemingly waiting for orders. Ray Malone had melted away like Rumpelstiltskin.

"First of all, Chloe, what do you know about the world of modelling?"

I opened my mouth and shut it again, then looked at Mum for support. There was none to be had.

"I hoped I'd find out something about it by coming here," I stuttered.

Serena Montague put her elegantly coiffured head to one side and said: "Good, good. It's always better to admit to knowing nothing. It makes my job a lot easier. First of all, Charlie here – who has very kindly agreed to take some snaps of you today, although he's supposed to be somewhere else – is going to take you down to our studio and I'm going to have a chat to your mum. Charlie?"

"Right. Sure. Come on, then, Chloe. Follow me. Got your gear?"

I grabbed my bag and hurried after him. There was something comforting about this big, bulky man with his cockney accent and dreadful clothes, especially after the plush elegance of Serena Montague's office and her cut-glass English. I shuffled after him into the studio. There were lots of lights on stands everywhere and a camera on a tripod pointed at a square of white canvas tacked against one wall.

Charlie called out to someone: "Cheers! This looks fine, Rob."

A tall, broad-shouldered, dark-haired boy of about my age, dressed in dirty jeans and T-shirt, was fiddling about with some sort of photographic equipment. He nodded at me shyly then went back to his work.

"What sort of music d'you listen to, Chloe?"

"Oh, any," I said. "As long as it's not boy-bands."

Charlie chuckled and I relaxed. "Well, that's fine, 'cos we ain't got no bleedin' boy-bands, 'ave we, Rob? Rob's my nephew, by the way. Working as my assistant at the moment. Here from Australia on his gap year, though why he needs a gap year God only knows. His whole life seems to have been one long bloody gap year as far as I can see. Kids these days." He shook his head in mock sorrow, before turning back to address me.

"Now, Chloe," he said. "All I want you to do is

follow instructions when I give them and when I don't give any instructions I want you to do what you feel is right, is that clear?"

I nodded.

"I'm just gonna test the light and then I want you to move to the music and I'll start shooting. Piece o' piss. You ready?"

As the music started up – he'd put on some Robbie Williams – all I could do was stand there, rooted to the spot. I felt like a prize prat. I had this huge urge to shout out that I'd changed my mind and it might be better if I left now, before I wasted any more of the agency's time.

"Just relax," Charlie called out. "Try tapping your feet."

Maybe because he sounded so encouraging and kind I began to loosen up a little. At his suggestion I began to tap my feet, and it wasn't long before I became caught up in the beat. *Just imagine you're out clubbing on a Saturday night*, I told myself firmly and closed my eyes. It did the trick.

Soon, the music enabled me to forget the camera entirely. With growing confidence I opened my eyes and danced for all I was worth, as Charlie snapped. Contrary to all my expectations, I was having fun. I could have danced for hours, but after a couple of tracks, the music faded.

"Good," Charlie said, when we'd finished this particular bit. "We might be able to use some of those for your T-card. Serena told you about that yet?"

I shook my head.

"It's your calling card, when you go for a job," he explained. He was changing cameras now and his nephew was dragging a stool up, presumably for me to sit on.

"Four-sided booklet thingy with your name on the front and different sorts of snaps of you. Full-length, close-up, some colour, some black and white."

I was told to go behind a screen then and change into the plain white T-shirt I'd brought along. That done – not without some nervousness on my part at the thought of stripping off with two men present – Rob motioned me silently to hop on to the stool.

"What d'you think of Serena?" Charlie asked me.

"Scary," I said. Charlie laughed and clicked the shutter.

"More front than Harrods, that one. Take no

notice of the accent. She's a barrer boy just like me, really. Now, Chloe, when I tell you to move your head to the left I want you to do it by slow degrees, is that understood? And I'm going to talk to you as I take these pictures. I need to know what kind of girl you are."

For the next twenty minutes I must have told him my entire life story. I was actually enjoying being the centre of attention. Charlie really seemed to be interested in my answers. More than that, he seemed to think I was funny.

"If you were a fruit, Chloe, what would it be?"

I hesitated. "A banana," I decided.

"Saucy!"

"I was talking about my personality," I said. "You need to peel away the skin before you discover who I really am."

Charlie snapped.

"And if you were an animal?"

"Last week I'd have said a jellyfish."

"Why's that, then?"

I felt it would be all too easy to give everything away to a man like Charlie. No doubt thousands of models had, and that was why he got good pictures.

"Nah! It's a bit complicated," I said, thinking of all the dithering I'd done in my life. "Now though, I think I'm starting to fit my name. Dove. Ready to fly." I stretched out my arms and Charlie snapped again.

"Great! Now, can you look as innocent as one?"

I put my knees together, crossed my hands in my lap and lowered my eyes. He snapped again.

"Ever been in love, Chloe?"

"Loads of times," I said. "But never with anybody real. I'm saving that one."

"Who's your ideal man, then?"

I didn't have to think too hard.

"Lord Byron," I said, "for one."

"What, that poet geezer who had it away with his own sister?"

I laughed. He snapped again.

"Mad, bad and dangerous to know," I reminded him.

"You wanna be careful of blokes like that. They can do your head in if you let them."

"What a way to go, though."

Charlie grinned. "Young girls these days. Now one last snap. Right. Rob, switch the lights back on, will you."

I blinked, unaccustomed to the light and Rob put out his hand to steady me as I clambered down from the school. I giggled at this unexpected act of courtesy and then I wished I hadn't as Rob turned bright red and looked at the floor.

"It's been a pleasure working with you," Charlie said. "Rob, would you escort this young lady back to Serena's office?"

Outside the door to Serena's office, Rob said, "You're honoured. Charlie McGrath's not always so nice to the girls he photographs."

His slight Australian accent was apparent now I'd finally heard him say more than half a dozen words.

I was stunned. Charlie McGrath? *The* Charlie McGrath, photographer of supermodels and royalty, politicians and film stars?

"What's Charlie McGrath doing photographing me?" I whispered.

"He and Serena go back years," Rob said. "She was stuck today so when she rang him he dropped everything. As he usually does whenever she snaps her fingers." He neither approved nor disapproved, clearly, but was just stating a rather obvious fact. "Gotta go now. Good luck. They'll be great piccies."

"Do you really think so?" I could feel myself blushing madly and hoped that Rob didn't think I was fishing for compliments.

"Honest," he said. "You'll see." Then he was gone.

The rest of the time with Serena passed by in a haze while she talked percentages and contracts with my mother. Then we were at the lift again and Serena was pressing the button with a blood-red talon.

"Now, you'll be hearing from us in a couple of weeks when we've chosen your pictures for your T-card, Chloe," she said. "We also need to choose some for the yearbook – that's the big black book you probably saw on my desk."

I nodded.

"That book contains photos of all the models we have on our books. You'll be in there too before long."

The lift arrived and we were bundled in, good-byes exchanged.

"Wasn't I supposed to sign something? I'm sure Dad said I'd have to read the contract very carefully before signing it."

"Didn't you listen to anything she said? It'll come

in the post," Mum said, more flustered than snappy. "They expect you to think carefully and take all the advice and time you need before you sign. It's not some cowboy operation this, you know."

By now we were on the ground floor and heading for the exit, out through the revolving doors and on to the street once more. Finally, I could start believing that my life was going to change. I was going to earn money – big money. Enough, anyway, to get my dad off my back whenever he went on about university and MY FUTURE. What could he do now if I decided I wasn't going to university – at least not next year anyway. Maybe I'd take a leaf out of that Rob's book and have a gap year – but mine would be spent modelling fabulous clothes and having a wonderful life.

"Chloe. You mustn't let this go to your head, you know," Mum said. She must have spotted the wild look in my eyes.

"How could I possibly do that with you and Dad around?"

"There's no need to be sarky," she said. "I'm just thinking how this will affect the rest of the family. Not just you."

"How?"

"Well, there's your sister for a start. It's hard for her following in your footsteps. You've already got loads more advantages than she has, and now this."

"Advantages? What advantages?" I couldn't think of anything I had that Lindsay would envy.

"Well, there's your figure and your good looks and your brains. You've never had to struggle like Lindsay does at school. Then there's her weight. I keep telling her it's only puppy fat, but you know what she's like."

I was stunned. Why had we never had this conversation before? I'd grown up thinking my sister was the favourite. She was always being praised, even when she didn't seem to have done anything to deserve it. I'd always assumed that my achievements, such as they were, counted for nothing.

But maybe I'd simply misunderstood. They thought I didn't need to be told that I was clever or good-looking, because they imagined I knew already. But I'd been comparing myself to Kelly — and next to her I'd felt gawky and plain. It had taken a stranger on the street to spot whatever qualities I possessed and to prefer them over Kelly's obvious girly prettiness. And it had taken a man with a camera to bring it out.

chapter eight

"Are you going to open it, then? Get her a sharp knife, Linds, or we'll be here for ever, she's all fingers and thumbs."

It was a few weeks later. The bulky package had been delivered while I was out earning a crust – pardon the pun – at the sandwich shop, and Mum must have been dying to get at it all day.

Feigning indifference, Lindsay strolled over to the breadboard and strolled back with the bread knife. If she could have taken a detour I swear she would have. From the living room, Dad's dreams shunted his snores towards the kitchen. Not even the arrival of his new seed catalogue would have got him up from the settee – his reserved spot for

Saturday afternoons.

"It's my portfolio," I said. "And my T-card by the look of it."

My heart was pounding as I withdrew the leather-bound book from the confines of its buff envelope and quickly scanned the letter that accompanied it.

"Charlie's done you proud," Serena had written. "The quantity isn't much, but I'm sure you'll agree that the quality is excellent."

There followed an acknowledgement of the contract I'd returned, signed, and how this meant that now we were ready to go and all that was left for me to do was to make sure I was available for go-sees as and when they turned up. She made everything sound so simple.

Mum was already pulling out chairs and rearranging them round the table so we could get the best view of the book.

It was clear, as soon as I set eyes on the first picture, that Charlie McGrath was no ordinary photographer. Like everyone else, I'd been snapped before – eyes screwed up and blinking against the sun or smiling a smile that had evolved into a grimace because the photographer had lost his bearings on the camera and kept me standing around too long.

Charlie McGrath was in a different league.

"My God," Mum breathed. "These are absolutely stunning."

"Don't be daft," I said, trying to sound cool, but I knew she was right. Lindsay still hadn't said anything, so I knew she must be pretty impressed too.

I remembered all those questions he'd asked while he snapped away. At the time I thought he'd just been trying to make me relax, but I saw now just what he'd been using my answers for.

There I was with my arms outstretched, explaining that I was ready to fly. Here I was, on the stool, looking straight ahead at the camera, hands folded demurely in my lap, knees together, long skinny legs and pigeon toes transforming me into a prim fifteen year old, innocent as my name.

Then there was a whole series of pictures showing me oblivious to everything as I danced around. How had he managed to make me look so lissom, and so incredibly wild and sexy and not goofy at all, I wondered.

My favourite was a shot of me looking waif-like, hunched in a corner, arms wrapped around my knees, two huge black smudges for eyes, pale-skinned, the mouth I'd always complained about looking bruised and tender and voluptuous.

There were sharp profiles and full-length shots, black and white, colour, even sepia. In one picture I was turning a cartwheel, caught for ever on camera just before I came down. Some of these pictures had been reproduced on my T-card and must have been hand-picked to show the different aspects of my personality. Or rather to show Charlie's genius, that could spot them and then interpret them for the camera.

"You look like a different girl in every shot," Mum said, her voice breathy with amazement.

Lindsay still hadn't spoken, which must have been the longest she'd ever lasted in the same room as me without passing a snide comment.

Now Dad was here, peering over my shoulder, face crumpled with sleep. He gave a low whistle and followed it with: "Bloody hell. Who's the pin-up?"

Lindsay tutted and called him a perv, and then Mum tutted and told her not to be so ridiculous, it was just a joke.

Only it wasn't a joke, because it was obvious

from the double-take he did that he'd actually – albeit briefly – thought these pictures were of someone else.

"Doesn't she look lovely?" Mum said.

"She looks like a tart," Dad said.

Lindsay sniggered while Mum gasped and I reeled from the shock of being labelled a tart by my own father. The nerve of the man!

"She does not. She looks just like the models in *Vogue*."

There was an edge to Mum's voice. She was well up for a row. Grim-faced and arms akimbo, she tapped one foot on the floor while Dad leafed through the portfolio, lingering over each shot and making various comments.

"Can't you see she's been set up? Look at this one! She looks like jail-bait. And here. Look where his camera's pointing!"

I was furious. *Of all the narrow-minded, self-righteous prudes*, I thought. I slammed the book shut and snatched it up from the table.

"This is cutting-edge fashion photography, Dad," I reminded him. "The bustle went out some years ago, and women have been showing their legs since the nineteen twenties. I'm sure you must be able to remember that far back."

Dad scowled and Mum suppressed a smirk. She reminded him that Charlie McGrath had photographed everyone from Twiggy to Madonna in his day and had a world-wide reputation.

"A world-wide reputation for what? Being a dirty old man?"

"Takes one to know one," I muttered.

"Happy families," Lindsay said, grabbing a handful of biscuits on her way out. "If you'll excuse me, I've got stuff to do."

Dad and I seemed to have reached stalemate. I couldn't understand why he was behaving like some Victorian *pater familias*. Usually he got into a right strop when politicians started talking about morality – and anyway, what was I exposing, for Chrissake?

"I would have thought," I said, "that you would be proud of me. Olympus is one of the leading agencies in the country, and it's not everyone gets their portfolio done by someone like Charlie."

"Oh, it's Charlie now, is it?"

"Like it or not, Dad, this portfolio means the start of my career as a model. Who knows where I could be in six months' time?"

"I hope you'll be swotting for your A levels and looking forward to taking up your university place."

"Oh, God, off we go again," I groaned.

Dad glared at me. I'd had enough. Now was the time to give it to him hot and strong. "Well, actually," I said, "I've been giving that idea some serious consideration, and I've pretty well decided I won't be taking up any offers of a university place next October – even if I'm offered one. In fact, I might not even bother with university the following year either, if the modelling takes off," I said.

Until I spoke the words, I'd never seriously considered jacking in my education all together. Serena Montague had been quite impressed when I'd told her that I'd applied for a place at uni to study English and Modern Languages and even said how nice it was to meet a girl who had her head screwed on, once in a while.

Was I allowing my success to run away with my common sense, I wondered. Although so far the only success I'd had was in totally pissing my father off. I thought he was going to explode. He has this vein just above his left eye that seems to take on a throbbing blue life of its own whenever he gets mad. Right now it was doing the salsa.

"Have you any idea about the kind of lifestyle you'll be getting into if you let yourself get carried away with this modelling business?" he demanded, his level voice belying his mad eyes. "Believe me, Chloe, it's not a world for young girls like you. Young models are two a penny, you must know that. You'll get chewed up and spat out before you know it, and it won't be as easy to pick up the pieces as you seem to think."

"Why can't you be pleased for me?" I wanted to know. "I'll be making money. I'll have choices. Isn't that what life's about? Or would you rather I was dependent on you for money all the time?"

I was trying to keep a check on my voice – I had no intentions of being accused of hysteria although I was near to tears. I swallowed hard and continued, determined to say everything I'd been wanting to say for ages and had never been in a position to. I persevered. This portfolio, my T-card and Serena's letter of congratulations had – for one brief, glorious moment – made me suddenly fearless.

"That's exactly what you do want, isn't it?" I said. "If I have to keep asking you for money, then you've got power over me, and if I don't do things according to your pathetic rules, then I can kiss goodbye to my allowance."

"Calm down, Chloe," Mum said. "Your dad only wants what's best for you."

"No, he doesn't. He wants what's best for *him*. What's easiest. What's safest. What he knows. Well, tough, because now I've got the chance of making some real money and that means I don't need to ask either of you for your approval!"

Now it was my turn to make an exit, and once I'd calmed down and replayed the scene in my head back in my room, I decided I'd been more than a match for Dad.

chapter nine

As soon as I knew both my parents and Lindsay would be out the next evening — a rare event indeed — I sent Kelly a text inviting her round, adding strict instructions to call into the off-licence en route. I felt flat, anticlimactic, and the only cure was a good old moan.

"So, still ordinary enough for a night in with your old mates, then?" she quipped, expertly flipping the top off a bottle of Archer's Aqua.

"Oh, God. Don't you start," I said. I launched into the row I'd had with my dad about my portfolio. "Trouble is he still thinks I'm about ten."

"Did you tell him even Afghan women have stopped wearing burkas?"

We both giggled and sipped at our drinks in companionable silence for a while. Any atmosphere there'd been between us lately, since my brush with Ray Malone and the model agency, seemed to have evaporated, much to my relief. Honestly, I couldn't have cared less about being top dog, but it had always been the most important thing for Kelly. She needed an audience, always had done. Normally I was happy to oblige. Could I help it if the tables had been turned for once?

After a while, Kelly said, "You're not serious about giving up the idea of uni next year, though?"

"Why not?" I said. "People do. There was this guy from Australia helping the photographer out at the agency. He's on a gap year."

"Oh yeah? Tell me more. Was he a hunky surfer? Did you give him your number?"

Kelly saw the possibilities for romantic liaisons everywhere she looked. I tried to tell her I'd barely noticed him, I'd been so overwhelmed by every-thing else that had been going on, but it was clear she didn't believe me.

"So when's it all going to start happening, then?" she went on. "I'd have thought you'd have had at least one job under your belt by now."

Her gaze drifted across to my portfolio, which Mum had been showing one of the neighbours earlier, much to my embarrassment and Lindsay's obvious irritation, but she made no attempt to pick it up. So, she wasn't over it, then.

"I'm trying not to think too much about it," I said. "Nice things only happen when you least expect them in my experience. Want another?"

Kelly could drink most people under the table and I'd long ago stopped trying to keep up with her. She took another bottle, with that look she has that says she's only drinking it because you've insisted and said, "You're not the only one waiting for something to happen, actually. Have you seen the ad for the college drama production?" She was suddenly animated again.

I hadn't but Kelly soon filled me in on the details. She said she was going for the main part.

"You're bound to get it," I said. "You'll walk it."

"Acting isn't as easy as you think, you know, Chloe," she said. "It's not like walking up and down a catwalk or staring at a camera."

I ignored the remark. When Kelly said things to

hurt I always told myself it was never deliberate. It was just the alcohol making her a bit lairy.

Outside, the wind had got up and heavy late autumn rain was battening against the Velux window above our heads.

I lifted my eyes, pulled a face and said: "Would you just listen to that. Makes you so want to book your summer holiday, doesn't it?"

Kelly was looking a bit shifty. "Actually, Chloe, I'm glad you brought that up," she said. "Someone in my drama class has an aunty who's got a villa in Greece somewhere. She's asked me to make up the party."

"Oh."

"The aunty's not going to be there, so there's no need to look so horror-stricken. It'll just be me, this girl from my drama group, a couple of her mates and any gorgeous Greeks who fancy improving their English."

I was gutted. What was going on here? Kelly and I had spent hours in the past fantasizing about what we'd do once A levels were out of the way, and we were finally free to do as we pleased.

"But – I thought we were going to travel round France together," I said, when I finally found my

69

voice again. I didn't even try to disguise how hurt I was.

Kelly was clearly uncomfortable with my distress.

"Oh, that," she said. "We-ell. I never really fancied it. All those ugly little French men. Now the Greeks are something else altogether. Besides, it was never a firm arrangement, was it?"

She drank the bottom half of her second Archer's in one go and reached for a third, clearly feeling in need of some Dutch courage while she continued to blag her excuses. "Anyway," she went on. "I kind of assumed you wouldn't be wanting to make any commitments – just in case you got whisked away to take part in London Fashion Week, or whatever."

"Don't be stupid," I said, sullen-voiced.

"No. Fair dos. It could happen." Kelly was still trying to make light of what she'd done. "This time next year you could be a millionaire. Look at Gareth Gates."

I watched her reach over and haul my portfolio up on to the table where she proceeded to flick through the pages, squinting at the photos in a slightly drunken manner. For a moment I wondered if she intended doing some damage to them. I had to check myself from reaching across and snatching the book back.

"Things have changed, Chloe. Surely you can see that?" She spoke like someone who'd been rehearsing her words carefully all afternoon.

"How do you mean?"

"Well, think about it. What happens if we book a flight to France, get the trip sorted out and everything? Then at the last minute you get offered some modelling job that pays five-hundred quid for a couple of days sitting around. What would you do? Turn it down because you've had a better offer? I don't think so."

Put like that she had a point. What would I do? The answer was blindingly obvious and we both knew it.

"Where would I be then?" she went on. "Surely you wouldn't begrudge me a summer in Greece with everything you've got to look forward to, would you?"

"Course not," I said, as nonchalantly as I could, watching her turn over the pages of my portfolio.

"Some of these are all right, actually," she said, like she couldn't have been more surprised.

71

Then she closed the book with a deft flick of her wrist and replaced it on the chair, and smiled at me as if everything between us was hunky-dory.

An entire month had passed since Mum and I had gone up to London. The welter of emotions I'd experienced on the way home had sustained me for weeks afterwards. But now the experience seemed so distant, it was like I'd dreamed the whole thing. Did I really have everything to look forward to, like Kelly said? From where I was sitting, I didn't even have a holiday or a best friend any more, let alone a fabulous career.

chapter ten

Lindsay had been off school all day with a so-called cold. When I got in from college — freezing cold and starving — I went straight to the kitchen and hit the bread bin. It didn't take me long to discover that she'd got there first and demolished practically a whole loaf, without even bothering to wipe away the evidence.

"Cheers, Linds, you greedy cow," I yelled at the top of my voice.

"What?" She dragged herself off the settee, where no doubt she'd been watching videos all day in front of a roaring fire — when she hadn't been hoovering up the contents of the fridge — and padded into the kitchen in her ridiculous pink fluffy slippers.

"What am I supposed to eat?" I brandished the heel of bread that remained. "Did it never occur to you to take another loaf out the freezer?"

She looked at me with that dense expression she conjures up whenever she feels hard done by. "What's your problem? Had a bad day, have we?"

"Well, I haven't been lying around on my fat arse all day stuffing my face, like some people."

"I've got a cold. You're supposed to feed a cold, aren't you?"

She sniffed theatrically to prove her point, then shuffled back into the living room on pink paws. I plunged the last slice of bread into the toaster and put the kettle on. Hot chocolate, that was what I needed. Something to comfort me after another day wandering round college on my own, pretending I wasn't bothered when people asked me if I'd met Kate Moss yet.

I wrapped my hands around my steaming mug and thought about lunchtime. Kelly, in the thick of her acting cronies, deigning to throw me a royal wave, but making no effort to come and join me. Well, she'd just been made star of the annual College Revue, so I'd heard. Why would she want to spend time with a model who'd not actually done any modelling yet?

"Oh, I forgot." Lindsay plodded back into the kitchen. "Your model thingy rang up. Something about a job. Can you ring back. Said it was urgent. Probably want you to model spot cream or facial hair remover."

"What! When was this? Why didn't you tell me sooner?"

I ran to the phone, dialled, and when someone answered asked to be put through to Serena Montague.

"Chloe, darling. How are you?"

I was about to reply but Serena didn't give me the chance. I was soon to learn that Serena Montague didn't do small talk. Time was money and polite requests after people's health made none.

"Now, you're going to be absolutely thrilled, Chloe, sweetheart, when I tell you that you have been selected to appear with three more of the agency girls in a pop video. Tough Love, the band's called. Heard of them?"

Her words floated into one ear, drifted around the empty space in my head for a while making absolutely no sense, then, having spectacularly failed to spark any connection with my brain, trickled out the other ear.

"Chloe? Are you there?"

"Yes," I said. But it came out hoarse, and sounded more like "S".

"It's in two weeks' time. You're going to have to get the day off college."

College? What college?

"No problem," I said.

"You'll be picked up at six in the morning. I know it's early but they're on a tight budget and they daren't risk the expense of going into two days."

She mentioned the name of the place being used for filming — some stately home north of where I lived. Then there was some stuff about money and about what an opportunity this would be for me to shine so early in my career. When she brought the conversation to a close with a curt goodbye, I was left staring down the phone, dazed, and positive I'd missed some vital bit of information, but too embarrassed to ring back and check.

Just to be on the safe side, on the day I took everything the agency had ever sent me, including my portfolio and a couple of T-cards. On the strength of this – my first assignment – I'd finally jacked in my job at the sandwich shop and celebrated by spending all my earnings on a huge black canvas bag, which was now stuffed full of all the make-up and hair products I possessed. I'd even packed my hairdryer.

I must have looked a complete amateur as I clambered up into the van, hauling my bag in after me to take up the last remaining space. Three pairs of eyes turned on me, each pair very different, but each, in its own way, staggeringly attractive.

The first person to speak possessed the most intelligent ones – vivid turquoise, flecked with brown. Although her brows were dark and heavy, her chin-length hair was white-blonde. Her mouth was full-lipped and unsmiling, and her square jaw gave her an aggressive quality.

"Going on your holidays?" she asked, thrusting out her chin as she spoke, and the others giggled.

I stared at the mole at the corner of her mouth and remembered something Charlie had said about every beautiful model having at least one flaw in her appearance. Perhaps if I fastened on this aspect of the girls I was to be spending the rest of my day with, then I'd get through it with some self-esteem left by the end of it.

"Honestly, Kendall, give the poor girl a chance. We haven't all been modelling since we were six months old."

The second girl – in sharp contrast to Kendall's East End twang – spoke as if she'd been educated at Cheltenham Ladies' College. But anyone less English-rose-looking would have been hard to find. She was dark-haired with skin the colour of baked cinnamon. I thought at first she must be Indian, but there was something about the way her nutmeg-brown eyes curved upwards that made me think maybe she had some Malay blood in her.

She smiled at me, an impish grin which immediately dispelled the illusion of some haughty exotic princess, and her face dimpled.

"Kendall used to do Pampers ads on TV, you know. But she was a brunette then. I'm Sofia, by the way, and this is Tillie."

The third person gave me a weak smile but didn't speak.

"Tillie's not good in the mornings," Sofia said. "Go back to sleep, darling, we'll wake you up when we get there."

Tillie adjusted the Walkman that was clamped to her head and lay back on her seat. In profile she was exquisite. There was something fragile about her that reminded me of a gazelle, with her long, slender neck and the smoky, smudgy eyes that were soon closed in sleep. Perhaps the feature that stood out most was her large, oddly lopsided, sulky mouth. *Another of Charlie's flaws?* I wondered. If it was a flaw it only made her appear more vulnerable.

I cast about for something to say but I could think of nothing that wouldn't make me look like an amateur. I reminded myself it was still only six o'clock in the morning. Neither Tillie nor Kendall seemed remotely interested in making small talk and even the immaculately-mannered Sofia had withdrawn her attention once I was strapped in and we were on the road again. Maybe the best thing to do was catch some Z's while I still could.

chapter eleven

I woke with a start. It was just about light now and we'd left the urban sprawl far behind. Nothing for miles but rolling moors dotted with dark trees, naked for the winter that out here in the wilds of the country seemed to have hunkered down already. Finally, we arrived at our destination and drove slowly up the drive. Statues — blackened by age and weather — lined both sides. The façade of the house swept into view, full of faded Gothic splendour. It wouldn't have surprised me if a skeleton had suddenly shown its skull at one of the upstairs windows.

"Blimey," Kendall said, as the driver pulled up and decanted us from the van. "Where's the bleedin' butler?"

She scrabbled in her bag for a cigarette, lit it and handed it over to Tillie. "You sure you're OK with this, babe? If there's any trouble. . ."

Tillie took the cigarette and drew deeply on it, as the two of them walked away almost out of earshot. I thought I heard Tillie say something like: "Gavin asked for me, didn't he? D'you think he'd ever use me again if I turned him down?"

Kendall shrugged. "I'm only thinking of your feelings, Tillie. It might be too much for you – him being here."

She put her hand on Tillie's arm but Tillie shrugged her away. "I got here first, remember?" she hissed. "Let him rearrange his life if he can't stand the idea of bumping into me. I'm not changing where I go and who I go with just to stay out of his hair!"

"OK, OK! Chill!" Kendall put up her hands in mock-surrender.

I was intrigued by their conversation but whatever was going on was clearly not for my ears. Then, Sofia's wild shrieks of delight distracted me.

"Oh, look! There's Gavin! Dah-ling!"

At the top of the steps that led to the entrance

of the house, someone was gesticulating wildly in our direction. Sofia ran towards the house and took the steps two at a time, waving madly. Tillie and Kendall followed in her wake, whatever it was they'd been in a huddle about put firmly on the back burner, at least for now. I trundled up behind, cursing the weight of my holdall as I dragged it up the steps.

"There'd better be breakfast laid on." This from Kendall.

"Briefing first, then food." Gavin – a small, slimly-built man of indeterminate age with the elegant walk of a dancer – pursed his lips and attempted a scowl to show who was in charge.

"No-oo. The loo first or I'll wet myself," Tillie insisted.

There were a number of others – presumably the crew – hovering about and braying at each other while simultaneously waving clipboards or mobile phones around. To a man or woman they were dressed in sharp black. Gavin called over one of the minions.

"Show these girls the loos, Victoria, dear, and then bring them straight back into my office. Oh, hello, my love." This last endearment to me. "You must be Chloe. I've been told I have to treat you with extra special care because it's your first time. It's not often I get to see a virgin in my job."

I blushed, mortified, as he pecked my cheek and winked at the others, who seemed to think his remark was the height of wit. "Don't let these minxes lead you astray," he said.

"It's the other way round, Chloe, darling," Sofia giggled. "This man is such a prima donna I'm surprised he can still get anyone to work with him."

It was clear that all this bitching was just a ritual. I envied them their easy familiarity. The new-girl feeling threatened to overwhelm me.

Gavin, hand on chin, scrutinized me intently. "Well, I must say Serena was right to take you on," he said. "I loved your portfolio and you'll be absolutely perfect for this video. You've got such a sixties face."

The new-girl feeling began to retreat. *You can do it*, I kept on telling myself, *or you wouldn't be here*. I remembered my mum's words on the train going up for my initial interview at the agency. This was just another hurdle. Over bacon butties and flasks of hot coffee – administered by yet more minions – we were finally put in the picture.

"The boys won't be here until midday – very rock 'n' roll – I know." He yawned, miming weary exhaustion, and the minions duly giggled. "You girls, meanwhile, have to get your hair and make-up done and then we'll sort out who's wearing what. All that'll be required of you after that is for you to practise your dancing until we do the shoot. You can all dance, I hope?"

Oh, I could dance all right. Finally, something I could relax about.

From Gavin's office we were shunted to another much larger room, which had been transformed into a hairdresser's-cum-beauty-salon for the day. There were clothes strewn everywhere and at least half a dozen full-length mirrors. There were plenty of electric fires too, to keep out the chill that rattled the lead-lined windows and crept down from the high ceiling. Here there were even more people, but this time they were people with a real purpose – hairdressers, make-up artists, dressers – far removed from the ones who'd descended on us initially, all full of their own importance as they tapped out text messages to each other and ran around in circles telling each other what to do.

One of them, a woman about my mum's age who looked reassuringly ordinary and not remotely rock 'n' roll, took my elbow and propelled me to a washbasin, where she sat me down and swathed the top half of my body in a fluffy white towel.

"I'm Joyce," she said, "and I'm in charge of your hair. I'm going to cut you a fringe and lop off a good couple of inches, then give you a few highlights. Gavin wants you all dressed up like dolly birds, as I'm sure he's said."

I nodded. Gavin had said a lot. Like how he'd moved heaven and earth to get the owners of the house to allow us to film there and if there was any damage he'd personally string up the person responsible. Like how all he wanted us to do was behave naturally and that if he liked something in rehearsal he'd ask us to do it again for the camera. The others had listened wearily and nodded as if he was stating the bleeding obvious. I'd nodded along with them, but much less convincingly, I'm sure.

As it turned out, the whole thing was a breeze. The costumes, hair and make-up completely transformed us. I wore an Alice band in my hair, and — like the rest of the girls — lashings of eye make-up and white, frosted lips. My outfit consisted of a jade green shirt with a ruffle down the front, a black and white checked miniskirt and knee-length white boots. Tillie was in a flimsy, floral dress, her hair in soft tendrils that cascaded to her shoulders, while Sofia, hair in pigtails, wore bell-bottomed trousers and a gauzy Indian-style top. Kendall was in hot pants, and the black peaked cap that hung low over her eyes gave her an incredibly sassy appearance.

"You look great," I risked saying, aware I might sound like a creep.

Kendall shrugged as if she already knew she did, and made me feel even more of a fool.

"Seen Tillie?" she asked, scanning the room.

Before I could reply she'd spotted her and flew over to the corner of the room where Tillie was standing peering into a glass of water, a look of yearning on her sad face.

Something was going on, that much I'd picked up. But whatever it was, I wasn't going to let it spoil my day. I was going to have fun.

chapter twelve

"You were terrific! Where did you learn to dance like that?"

I was on a high. Knocking back glass after glass of water from the cooler in the corner of the room, I needed to cool off after all that dancing.

For the first time that day, I made myself focus on the speaker. I'd been too nervous of the cameras to concern myself with the antics of the five boys who'd been performing their single "Be The One" on the makeshift revolving stage, while we girls had been doing our best to smile and look happy and bouncy for take after take.

Now that it was over, though, I was going to give this one my full attention – because he was gorgeous. Not tall — but then that was my own fault for being such a giant — but certainly not short, either, and with an air of confidence that made him appear bigger than he was.

"Thanks," I mumbled. "But I wasn't doing anything really."

I wanted to say that what I'd done was nothing compared with the performance they'd just given, but actually, since they'd only been miming, that would have been a lie. Instead I said something about how difficult it must be to mime convincingly.

He shrugged off my compliment. "Can't stand it," he said. "Being on stage. Now that's when you get the buzz."

I studied him further as he spoke. Eyes, deep set, dark and scarily sexy. Just the right amount of stubble on his chin. Razored hair that a fraction shorter or longer wouldn't have worked, but as it was worked to perfection. If I'd been hot after the dancing, I was even hotter now.

"You haven't told me your name."

I liked the way he said what he wanted to say, and with the minimum number of words.

"Chloe Dove," I said.

Immediately I was overcome with embarrassment because I felt I should have known his. After all, I was only part of the apparatus. He was the big draw. But if he sensed my shame he didn't let on.

"Greg Geffen," he said.

"I know," I replied, grateful for the let-out.

The ghost of a smile flitted across his angular face. "Liar," he said. "You'd never heard of us until today. But don't worry, this time next month we'll be a household name."

Such supreme self-confidence would have been unbearable if it hadn't been followed by another smile.

"The publicity people are here for an interview with the boys," Gavin yelled above the excited chatter that had broken out as soon as the final take had been passed. "So everyone else can get out of their stuff and start thinking about going home."

"I guess that means you." Greg spoke the words wistfully. "Just as we were getting on so well."

One of the minions pushed by, and Greg leaned over to speak to her. "Give us a lend of your pen, will you, love?" he said.

Flustered, the girl handed it over and waited.

"It's only a pen," he said. "No need to wait

around. You'll get it back later."

It was clear the girl had been dismissed. I watched her scuttle away, her face bright red. It flashed through my mind that she would have been me once.

"You can't get the staff these days," Greg quipped. I floated on a cloud of exhilaration. I was on the inside – with Greg – looking out, and it was definitely the place to be.

He grabbed my arm and started to scribble a number on my hand. The way he removed the top of the pen and stuck it in his mouth while he wrote made me feel like I was about to drop down dead on the spot.

"Call me, Chloe. You will, won't you?"

He leaned over and kissed my cheek. He smelled of make-up, and something spicy and expensive mingled with the faintest whiff of salty sweat. As I opened my eyes again Kendall was staring straight over at us from the other side of the room, chin thrust forward, turquoise eyes glinting danger-ously. She was furious, that was for sure. I blinked and lowered my eyes. This girl was scary.

Then someone grabbed Greg and hauled him away, more or less at the same time as one of the dressers pounced on me and ordered me to hurry along to the changing room. When I turned round to say goodbye, Greg was no longer there.

Later, in front of the mirror in the loos, I studied my new look. This time yesterday, Greg would never have looked at me twice. But I'd been transformed by the expertise of the dresser, the make-up girl and the hair stylist and now I was an object of desire.

I relived our encounter, still savouring his touch and the thrill of his lips as they brushed my cheek. I couldn't remember anything he'd said, yet his voice still rang in my ear. It was as if he'd put a spell on me. When he'd looked at me it was like he was offering me a challenge. Himself.

The clatter of the door behind me jolted me back to the present. It was Kendall. "Van's leaving in ten minutes," she said. "Without you at this rate."

"Just coming," I muttered.

She didn't move but hung around, half in and half out the door. I decided to let her wait a bit longer. Singing to myself – "Be The One", naturally – I filled the basin nonchalantly, pumped liquid soap into my hands, while covertly inspecting her reaction in the mirror, then plunged both hands into the water. But my moment of triumph was short-lived. I watched aghast as the writing on my hand began to blur before it finally disappeared for ever. I did my best to suppress a howl of dismay. I couldn't believe how stupid I'd been! In my determination to show Kendall I wasn't going to let her get to me, I'd just washed away Greg's telephone number! If it hadn't been so tragic it would have been hilarious.

"You all right?"

I wasn't going to broadcast my stupidity.

"Water too hot for me," I bluffed, drying my hands perfunctorily on a paper towel, before tossing it into the basket.

"Believe me, this is nothing compared to what you've got coming."

"Meaning?" She held the door open for me and I sailed through.

Since this morning, when I'd felt such a fool lugging that stupid canvas bag into the van, and feeling almost sick with nerves about the day ahead, I'd undergone a sea change. Maybe it was the expensive and exquisitely-made clothes that had transformed the way I felt about myself. Or the care lavished on me by the girl who'd done my make-up, and the lovely Joyce who'd done my hair and treated me like someone who'd been modelling all her life. Then there was Gavin, who'd been nothing but encouragement and praise. On top of everything there'd been Greg Geffen. If I fancied him, then he certainly fancied me. *Come on girl*, I told myself, with steely determination. *Don't let her walk all over you.*

"Jealous, are we?" I asked her. "There's really no need to be, you know. We were only exchanging phone numbers."

We were striding down the steps to the van now. The van driver beeped his horn and I could see Sofia waving at us from inside.

"Jealous over Greg Geffen?" Kendall sneered. "Don't make me laugh."

"Well, that's just dandy, then," I said, managing to reach the van just seconds before Kendall and opening the door for her. "After you."

chapter thirteen

One day I'm poised for flight, quivering with certainty that in Greg Geffen I have met my Destiny. Next, I'm sitting round the kitchen table with my family, eating Sainsbury's sausage rolls, blowing out candles and peeling shop-bought icing off my eighteenth birthday cake.

"Come on, Chloe, cheer up," Mum said. "You've been really miserable since you came back from that modelling job."

"Have you never heard of the word anticlimax?" I grumbled.

Lindsay stopped shovelling cake into her mouth for long enough to say that she'd always thought anticlimax was two words. I glared at her. She wasn't exactly in my good books at the moment.

"Why don't you get lost and have another go at trying to find where you put that box of chocolates you say you bought me," I said.

"I think you should give your sister the benefit of the doubt, Chloe," Mum said, anxious as always these days, it seemed to me, to back Lindsay up. "It's quite possible it happened like she said, you know. That she put them down somewhere at school and someone took them."

"I DID buy you a box of chocolates. I just took my eye off them for a minute and when I looked again they'd disappeared."

"Oh, yeah? I bet I can guess where, too." I puffed out my cheeks to indicate I was pretty sure she'd scoffed the lot before she'd even got them home.

Lindsay went bonkers then. "I haven't eaten them! Mum, will you tell her!"

"The lady doth protest too much methinks," I quoted, as she went running from the room, bawling loud enough to break the sound barrier.

I helped myself to another piece of cake while Mum looked on, grim-faced.

"Happy now?" she said. "How old are you today, eighteen or eight?"

"Come off it, Mum, you know as well as I do she's eaten them. If I go into her room now and look underneath her bed I bet I can even produce the empty box." Once more, I was the villain of the piece. And on my birthday, too!

"Why do you always have to stick up for her all the time?"

Mum shook her head sadly, as if she were addressing one of her little Year Fours she'd just caught defacing a book.

"Just think about it, Chloe," she said. "Here you are – eighteen years old today and everything in front of you. You've been in a video that very soon all the kids in the country are going to be bombarded with on every TV programme produced for their age group. You're doing well enough at college, even though you do the minimum you can get away with—"

Here I attempted a protest, but Mum shushed me and carried on with the lecture.

"You look great, and ever since you did that video – well, it's like. . ."

"Like what?"

Mum didn't usually scratch about for words like this.

"Well. It's like you've turned into a swan overnight."

"Cheers, Mum. You saying I was an ugly duckling before?"

Mum scowled and pushed her hair out of her eyes irritably. "Don't be ridiculous, Chloe. You know that's not what I meant at all," she said. "Stop fishing for compliments and try comparing yourself with Lindsay. There she is — struggling at school like you never did and on top of that she's just started her periods. All sorts of things are going on in her body and she's finding it really difficult to come to terms with the changes."

"We all get periods," I grumbled. "Some of us just get on with it."

"And some of us forget how awful all that stuff is until you get used to it," Mum snapped. "You for one can afford to be a bit more understanding and generous with all the good fortune you're having lately."

What good fortune? I asked God or whoever was up there. Seemed to me like just about everything that could go wrong was going wrong. When I'd tried to get Greg's number I'd been blocked every time, for one thing. When I'd tried to explain that

I was one of the models he'd worked with on the video shoot, some horrid little jobsworth from the production company had sneered at me: "Forget it! That's what they all say." Then she'd slammed the phone down on me. Meanwhile I relived the moment of our first and only meeting, edited the script, wrote the sequel. Except Greg Geffen was clearly not that interested in a sequel, or he would have done something, anything, to find me again.

I was beginning to think that life was more frustratingly, jaw-crunchingly, achingly boring now than it had ever been before I'd been so-called "discovered". After all, back then I'd had no hopes. No one had called me remarkable, no one had treated me like royalty, no one had made me believe that they had fallen in love with me. I'd been plain old Chloe Dove – you know, the lanky one who goes about with Kelly Driscoll.

My disillusionment was set in concrete by the last day of term. It wasn't just the fact that I hadn't heard from Greg, as if that wasn't bad enough. It seemed the agency had forgotten all about me too.

"The trouble nowadays is that you kids want everything to happen at once."

It was breakfast time in the Dove household and

my dad, sick and tired, so he said, of seeing me mooching around with a long face, was going off on one.

"You can't expect to be inundated with modelling jobs before you've been in the business more than two minutes. You have to give things a bit of time."

I was leafing through Lindsay's *Sugar*, not particularly listening. What would you know, I was tempted to say, a man who was still waiting for promotion to Head of Department even after twenty years had gone by and he'd been passed over three times in favour of someone younger and more dynamic?

"Anyway, with A levels so close perhaps you're better off concentrating on those."

"You're playing our song," I said, and yawned in a way I hoped Dad would interpret as being heavy with irony.

The caption jumped out at me immediately I turned the page, and saw Greg and the rest of the boys posing hunkily for the camera.

TOUGH LOVE. THE NEXT BIG THING.

"Ohmygod!" I screamed and practically knocked over my mug of tea.

"Bit old for that sort of stuff, aren't you?"

I swatted Dad away and continued to read. "TOUGH LOVE's first single — BE THE ONE — hits the shops at the end of January. Catch them on tour and check out their brilliant soon-to-be-released video. Turn to page twelve for more pics and all the low-down on the five guys who are about to take Britain by storm."

I flipped forward a few pages to more pictures of the boys, airbrushed to tanned perfection, each — apart from Greg who was looking mean and moody — flashing a set of blindingly white teeth. There was a little potted biography about each of them, but there was only one person I was remotely interested in.

"Greg Geffen is twenty-one years old, with the voice of an angel, the sense of humour of a demon and the looks of a demi-god."

Who writes this crap? I wondered. There was more. About how he'd dreamed of having a number one from the age of seven. About his favourite food: steak, rare. Favourite colour: black. Favourite time of day: night. Ideal woman: some-one as independent as himself and who knew what she wanted from life. *ME, Greg*, I wanted to scream.

IT'S ME YOU'RE LOOKING FOR!

I stared at Greg's picture for ages, trying to equate the face in the photo with the one I remembered, but I couldn't quite piece it together. This feigned sexuality was a pose, a tease for the camera. Kids' stuff. But when he'd looked at me it had been the real thing. X-rated.

"Get off my magazine!" Lindsay bore down like a wrathful gnome and snatched it from my hands.

"And a very good morning to you, too," I said. Since my telling-off from mum on my birthday I'd decided to be icily polite to Lindsay and to forbear from insulting her. But I couldn't keep the gloating note from my voice when I said:

"This one in the middle – Greg – he's much better looking in real life, you know."

Lindsay's mouth dropped open. "What? You mean it was Tough Love whose video you were in? You never said it was them."

I smiled demurely. "Well, you know me and boy-bands. Can't remember what any of them are called. They all sound exactly the same to me."

Lindsay was still staring at the photo, mesmerized.

"You just said they were some boy-band or

other. All this time and you didn't tell me who. All my class are talking about them. How could you have forgotten their name?"

I shrugged. So I'd forgotten the name of the band. But the name of Greg Geffen was carved on my heart.

chapter fourteen

I didn't normally get post, apart from the usual
junk mail or reminders from the library that my
books were overdue. But one day, the week before
Christmas, the postman brought a bonanza crop. I
was certain that the handwritten card with the
London postmark was from Greg. He'd finally
come to his senses, rung the agency and pleaded
with them to hand over my address.

Great handwriting, I decided. Firm, masculine,
dashing, with letters leaning slightly to the right,
clearly drunk with delight that finally the two of us
would be reunited. Hands shaking, I finally opened
the envelope and flipped immediately to the inside
of the card to read the message, even before I'd

properly registered the picture on the front.

"Hope you have a great Christmas and all you want for the New Year, Rob."

Rob? Rob? I flipped back to the picture. A surfing scene, only the surfer was Santa Claus in a wet suit. Very funny. There was a PS. *Off to stay with Scottish relatives to find out what this Hogmanay malarkey is all about. How's the glam world of modelling? Maybe we can catch up in the New Year.* A mobile number followed.

Rob. Of course, Charlie McGrath's Australian nephew over here in his gap year. How sweet of him to remember me! I remembered how kind and encouraging he'd been the day I went to have my portfolio pictures done. Seemed like men were like buses when you were a model, coming along in pairs like this. I couldn't help being disappointed, though, that the card hadn't turned out to be from Greg. If Rob McGrath could ferret out my address from the agency, then how come Greg Geffen couldn't?

Because he's forgotten all about you, a little voice whispered in my ear. I told the little voice to get lost and picked up the second card – which also had a London postmark, although this time my name and address had been typed rather than hand-written. This one was Greg's card, I decided. Absolutely definitely.

It wasn't. It was an invitation. A date. A time. A place. Not a Christmas card from Greg at all. Mortification pierced me like shards of glass. The little voice returned, only this time it had brought the whole gang along. *Listen, kid, forget it*, they chorused. *You're not in his league. He was just flirting with you.* But then one of the little voices told the rest to pipe down. *Hang on*, it said, *ignore this lot. Read it again. Read it again. Read it again.* I did.

In three weeks' time the video was being launched and this was my invitation to be there to see it, and to bring a friend along. It was going to be a huge event. Press, TV, radio, the works. And Greg. Finally, finally I would see Greg again. Hugging the invitation to me, I resolved that if Father Christmas never brought me another present I'd die happy.

There was a hastily scribbled PS from Serena.

It read: *Don't dress or make up at home. You'll be expected to wear the clothes you wore for the shoot, and people will be on hand to do your hair, etc. There'll be a car to meet you and bring you home. Have fun! S.*

Oh, wow! How cool would that be! I imagined all the neighbours out in force to witness the spectacle of yours truly being swept away in a stretch limo by a chauffeur in uniform. Lindsay would die of a jealous fit!

When I'd calmed down I opened my other post. Like most people I have a horror of anything that looks official, so I decided to leave the letter till last and opened the third card. It was from Kelly, and as well as a Christmas card it contained a reminder of the production she'd be starring in the following term. At the bottom of the card she'd written: *Tickets not ready yet but I'll get one for you as soon as they're done. I might get snapped up by a theatrical agency, you never know!!! PS AM I FORGIVEN FOR GREECE?*

I hadn't seen Kelly for ages. Oh, we'd said hello to each other in passing but she was always dashing off to rehearsals and I was never comfortable with the thespian crowd she seemed to be hanging about with more and more these days.

The last time we'd met up had turned out to be a bit of a disaster. But maybe that was as much my fault as Kelly's, for assuming she'd always be around for me. She was right to say I shouldn't stand in her way if she wanted to go off to Greece with some other mates. Maybe she'd been right too when she'd said she'd only made those other arrangements because she'd assumed I'd be doing more exciting things. I'd already had a taste of making easy money, and if more jobs like that came my way then how would I be able to turn them down in favour of a month's backpacking round France?

I should be big enough to make the first move, see things from Kelly's side. For as long as anyone could remember my rôle in her life had always been that of her sidekick. I'd never been under any illusions otherwise. She'd realized — even before I had, obviously — that I could no longer be expected to play it, now that I'd been snapped up by a top-class model agency.

I would invite her to the launch party, that's what I'd do, just to show her there were no hard feelings. As I opened my official-looking letter I suffered a twinge of conscience. If I didn't invite Kelly, who would I invite instead? The truth was that while she could summon countless friends at the click of her fingers, I couldn't. So who was doing who a favour here?

But when I clapped eyes on the huge cheque from the accounts department at the agency I stopped feeling sorry for myself, and when the very next day I got a call from Serena offering me my second assignment, I was back on cloud nine.

"It's only catalogue work this time," she informed me. "But it pays well."

If she'd told me I'd been booked to model oven chips I'd have jumped for joy.

On a high and feeling generous I rang Kelly that same evening to thank her for the card she'd sent me, and to invite her to the video launch party.

"Honestly, Chloe, I'm just so-o busy with rehearsals at the moment that I'm not sure if I can really afford to take the time out," she said. "It's not just the Revue, you know. I've got an interview coming up, and I have to rehearse a piece for that."

"Aw, come on, Kelly. I've got loads to tell you."

Talk about playing hard to get. She didn't even ask me what. We went backwards and forwards like this for ages.

"That's another thing. I've got to spend money on an interview outfit in the sales. I don't know about party stuff too. What are you going to be wearing?"

I avoided answering that one. I'd tell her on the night, I decided.

"Come on, Kelly. You can get round your dad, can't you? We'll make an evening of it," I suggested. "I'll have the Bacardi Breezers on ice."

Finally she began to thaw. "D'you think there'll be anyone there who could help my career?" she asked.

"Well, I expect there'll be agents and impresarios and people like that," I said. "You might nab a boy-band member too, if you're lucky."

As long as you keep away from the one I've got my eye on, I didn't say.

She thought a bit then said, quite chirpy now, "Yeah, go on then. You're right. Dad'll cough up for the suit when I tell him it's for an interview. Then if I get the cheapest thing I can find I can put the rest of his money with mine and buy a really nice dress for this thing of yours."

"That's my girl," I said.

chapter fifteen

To say that my next foray into the world of modelling was nothing particularly glamorous was possibly the understatement of the century.

What it meant, on that freezing, wet December morning, was getting up at sparrow fart and cycling to the train station to catch the first commuter train, being forced to stand for the best part of the journey, then spending another hour on public transport getting to the other end of London.

By the time I arrived I was cold, hungry and pretty damp. This time there was no red carpet — in fact there was no carpet at all, only dirty cracked lino and hard chairs I seemed to spend most of the day sitting around on, waiting, always waiting for the next thing to happen, and never once being informed what that next thing was.

All the other models had brought something to read, as well as flasks and sandwiches, not to mention warm, sensible dressing gowns they could seek refuge in while we hung around for hours on end in the draughty corridor, waiting for our call. *Chalk it up to experience*, I told myself, as I climbed into a pair of skimpy purple shorts that might have looked great in Falaraki but did little to promote the party spirit in me.

But finally it was over and I could go home, remembering to hand over a couple of T-cards to a bored-looking personal assistant on my way out. Another hour-long struggle to reach the station, followed by a wait of half an hour because I'd just missed the fast train, before finally securing a window seat on the next, which, typically, turned out to be the stopping train.

Not that I had the slightest intention of letting the truth get in the way of the scintillating account of the day I made sure I gave my parents and Lindsay when eventually I did reach home. The last thing I wanted was to have to listen to my dad going on about how I might be starting to have second thoughts and about how he wouldn't think any less of me if I decided to go back to the sandwich shop!

Finally, the BIG NIGHT arrived. Kelly, her hair glossier and blonder than ever, made her entrance wedged into a dress so tight my mum's eyes almost popped out with disbelief. She'd gone a bit overboard on the fake tan, but then she'd never had much truck with the natural look, and tonight she was clearly out to create a stir. The first thing she did was sweep the entire contents of my desk aside to make room for her make-up kit.

"Where's the booze, then?" she asked me.

I put my finger on my mouth to shush her and pointed to the door. I had a feeling Lindsay would be lurking outside, ready to sneak to Dad at the first opportunity.

She turned up the volume on my CD player in order to deaden the sounds of bottles opening and drink being poured. We giggled conspiratorially, already in the party mood.

"You look great in that dress," I said.

She did a twirl. "You don't think it's a bit – you know – obvious, do you?" she asked me.

I did, but it was more than my life was worth to say so. "If you've got it, flaunt it," I said instead, and Kelly was more than chuffed with that. "Tonight's going to be gre-at," I added, and danced round the room, glass in hand.

Kelly started to join in, but, one eye on the seams of her dress, thought better of it.

"I thought you could do my make-up," she said. Then, "If you fancy it, I mean."

It seemed to me that Kelly was really making an effort to be less bossy than she usually was.

"Yeah. Sure. I've learned some really great new tricks with the other models I've worked with, if you'll let me try them out."

"I've been using make-up on stage since I was five," she said. "But if you think you can teach me something new, go ahead."

She sat down in front of the mirror, the trace of irritation in her voice at odds with her pretty smile.

"I never said. . ." I began, but thought better of it and instead reached for a white towel and slipped it round her neck. Why did Kelly think I was in competition with her all the time?

After ten minutes I'd finished. Kelly squinted

into the mirror and pulled a face.

"I'm not sure this is a good look for me," she said.

I protested. "But this is the look, Kelly. Subtle, fresh, young and dewy-eyed."

"Well, I think it's shite. Give us a tissue, will you. I'll do it myself. You can't see I've got any make-up on at all from here."

As I handed her a box of tissues I felt like shaking her. Was she behaving like this just to spite me? Now she was slapping on colour with such enthusiasm she made Kat from Eastenders look like Ophelia's corpse. Well, if she wanted to look like a tart it was no skin off my nose.

"Anyway, don't you think you should be getting a move on? You've not even got your dress on yet, let alone any make-up," she said, giving her cheeks an extra dusting just to be on the safe side.

Why hadn't I told her when I had the chance? Thin-lipped, Kelly watched me struggle through my explanation.

"I should have guessed, I suppose," she sniffed. "It is your job, after all."

Fortunately, before anything could be said to make the situation worse, Lindsay stuck her head round the door to say the car was here.

"Ooh — what sort?" Kelly wanted to know.

"Only a white stretch limo with a chauffeur in uniform at the wheel."

"Wheeeeee!" we both yelled, finally fully united in our enthusiasm.

"You all right, Kelly? You look as if you've been Tangoed."

Trust Lindsay to open her big mouth and say exactly what I'd been trying not to say all night.

"Well, at least I'm not bursting out of my jeans!" Kelly peered at Lindsay as if she was seeing her for the first time. "What's happened to you since I last saw you?"

"Oh, that's Lindsay's diet," I explained. "She's been on and off it since Christmas. This must be an off week."

Lindsay glared at me. "You know it's impossible to lose weight before a period," she explained. "It'll drop off me next week. Five pounds at least. Besides these jeans shrank in the wash, remember."

"Oh, yeah? And the rest," I said, with a theatrical wink at Kelly.

Lindsay's diet — which she'd sworn she'd embarked on after the annual Christmas binge —

was entirely baffling to me, and boring beyond belief. Whenever she could nowadays she talked about calories and fat content – and when she got on to the subject of the dreaded water retention you'd soon find yourself losing the will to live unless you made a quick getaway. Now was the time to do just that, I decided, before she got any further down the track.

"I wish I could come with you," she said, enviously, as Kelly and I sashayed down the drive towards the car.

I laughed. "Sorry, but this is strictly for the grown-ups. No little scroats allowed. Especially no FAT little scroats."

For a moment Lindsay looked like she might be going to cry and I could have kicked myself for being so nasty, especially when Kelly giggled: "Honestly, Chloe, you can be worse than me at times."

"It's only a joke," I said, lamely. "She shouldn't be so sensitive. She's turning into a diet bore and needs to be told to shut up about it."

We clambered into the car and any thoughts I might have entertained about hurting my little sister's feelings evaporated immediately as I absorbed the fragrant ambience and sank into the plush upholstery.

All I could think about now, as the car purred down the dark suburban street before picking up speed, was Greg. Would he be on his way yet? I wondered. I prayed he'd be just as desperate to see me as I was to see him.

chapter sixteen

Much to Kelly's disappointment we were taken round the back way to the hotel.

"But I wanted to wave at the fans," she said. "Sign a few autographs in case they mistake me for someone from Eastenders."

"Who? Dot Cotton? Besides there's no one here yet."

That wasn't strictly true. I'd noticed a few sorry-looking girls – whose collective age couldn't have added up to double figures – hanging around on the pavement in front of the hotel as we swung down a side street and pulled up outside a less glamorous entrance.

"Chloe Dove?"

A woman stepped out of the shadows and flashed some sort of ID at me. I recognized her as one of the minions from the video shoot. She pushed through the doors and turned left down a corridor that smelled of stale food.

"This way please." Kelly made to trot along with her, but the minion wasn't having any.

"Someone will come and get you in a minute and take you to the bar," she said, placing herself firmly between us. "Strictly limited numbers in the dressing rooms."

Kelly looked even more put out when some great hairy bouncer with a bow tie and a shiny suit appeared from nowhere and offered to escort her. She threw me a look of desperation.

"It'll be fine," I reassured her. "Just go and enjoy yourself. I'll see you later."

If I knew Kelly, by the time I saw her again she'd be in the middle of the dance floor with a bloke in tow.

"Hurry along, Chloe," the minion ordered. "We're running late."

The dressing room was buzzing with activity. Hairdryers hummed, music blared and voices rose in excited chatter. Occasionally, a cork popped and cheers broke out above the general hum. The air was heavy with clashing perfume and the smoke from French cigarettes. I breathed it in, my eyes closed, unable to get enough of it. I was enraptured by the sheer theatricality of it all. It was like last time, at the shoot, I decided, but oh, so much more thrilling – because the moment held a much bigger promise than last time. Somewhere in this throng was Greg.

"Chlo-eee!"

Someone approached me from behind and covered my eyes with their hands. It was Tillie, dressed in costume and wearing full make-up, eyes shining and grinning broadly with that fabulous mouth. Sofia was right behind her, her hair in rollers but still managing to look as stunning as the heroine of a Bollywood movie.

"Isn't it absolutely great, darling!" she squealed. "All together at last! Kendall's over in that chair getting her make-up done."

They exchanged friendly waves, but as soon as I lifted my own hand in salute, Kendall turned her head and began to talk to her hairdresser. What *was* her problem?

"You'd better hurry up, Chloe!" Sofia continued.

"There'll be speeches soon and then they're going to show the video. Plus they want us to have our photos taken just before they run it!"

Sofia's sing-song voice with its perfect diction rose above the background chatter.

"How cool is that!" Tillie, swaying slightly and still grinning inanely, grabbed my hand and led me over to the cluster of make-up girls. Her mood was as different from the last time we'd met as it could be. Then, she'd barely been able to summon up enough energy to acknowledge me. Now, she was my new best friend. But, hey! I could live with it! I needed all the friends I could get at the moment, what with the lovely Kendall plainly cutting me dead from the other side of the room, and Kelly next door, no doubt fuming to herself that I'd ditched her deliberately.

But things were too exciting to dwell on the negatives. Somewhere in this building was Greg, I kept on reminding myself, and it was only a matter of time. . . Soon I was ready, too, and we were marshalled along another corridor. Tillie and Sofia giggled and joked as we pressed our way forward, pushing each other now and again for no reason I could think of, and setting off further waves of hilarity. Kendall played no part in their merriment but was as aloof as I remembered her. It was only when the doors swung open to admit us into the huge ballroom where the party was already in full swing that she permitted herself a professional smile, which she held while cameras snapped and people standing by applauded.

I looked out on to a sea of blurred faces, blinking each time a camera flashed. All this razzmatazz for a bunch of model girls, I couldn't help thinking. The world had gone mad! I scanned the horizon for Kelly but couldn't see her anywhere. Someone was making an announcement about it being time to watch the new video from soon-to-be-top-of-the-charts band, Tough Love. Once again we were being herded to another part of the room where huge screens were in place against the walls — I counted three in all. In spite of myself I was charged with the electricity of the occasion. Me, on widescreen TV! Tillie nudged me and grinned, and I grinned back.

"Isn't it exciting?" she said. "Will you watch with me?"

I nodded and moved over in the crush to let someone in. Tillie's broad grin faded to nothing.

"Oh," she said. "It's you. Look, there's someone over there I haven't seen for simply ages. Maybe I'll see you later, Chloe."

Then she was gone, leaving me spinning with amazement at the way I'd been so unceremoniously dropped, and the speed of her departure. Clearly Tillie was the type who thought she never had to explain anything.

"So why didn't you ring me? Did you take a vow of silence?"

"Greg."

He was really there, standing right next to me, clutching a glass of champagne, even better-looking than I remembered.

"Here, for you."

I took the glass and thanked him, certain I was scarlet with pleasure.

"So what happened?" he whispered, as the room grew dark and silence fell.

I explained the circumstances in which I'd lost his number, much to Greg's amusement.

"And I bet when you rang the production company their lips were sealed," he said. "Bunch of jobsworths."

"They were protecting you, I suppose," I started

to say as the video suddenly flashed on to the screen, drowning out my words. For the next three minutes there was nothing but the music, the dancing, Tough Love and a bunch of gyrating dancers.

And then it was over. There was applause and whistling and huge cheers, the lights were back on and the screens mysteriously disappeared.

"Didn't we look great together?" Greg said.

I must have drunk my champagne rather too quickly. Either that or Greg's proximity and the touch of his hand on mine as he offered to get me another was making me swoon.

"We looked fantastic," I said.

A waiter in a white jacket swept by, holding a tray of drinks aloft. Expertly, Greg replaced my empty glass with a full one.

"A toast, what do you think?"

I took the glass. "Where's yours? I can't toast on my own."

"Never touch the stuff," he said with a grimace. "Besides, I don't need alcohol to feel this good."

I felt myself blushing, convinced I must be in a dream. Next to Tillie or Sofia or Kendall, how could I possibly compare? What on earth did he see in me?

"To a number one," I said and raised my glass.

"And to you and me." Without taking his eyes off me he watched me drink until my glass was empty. It was the X-rated stuff again, that much was clear.

For the rest of the evening he stayed by my side, cutting people dead when they looked as if they might be about to approach him and engage him in conversation. Whenever I tried to move on, protesting that I really should try and find Kelly, he would distract me.

"What's she like, this Kelly?" he asked me, the third time I tried to cut away.

"About five five, blonde, bubbly, wearing a silver dress," I said.

When his face expressed mild interest I felt jealousy stirring inside and I regretted not telling him she was a complete dog.

"Well, in that case what does she need you hanging round her for? She's probably pulled by now."

I had to admit it seemed a plausible explanation. Besides, right now, the last thing I wanted to do was leave Greg's side.

"Look the other way," he said, as someone else approached. "That's Buzz Longhi, my manager. He'll be telling me I have to circulate if I give him the slightest bit of encouragement." He hailed a passing waiter to dispose of my champagne flute and his water glass. "Come on, let's dance. I want to know if you're as good at the smoochy stuff as you were with the other stuff up on that screen."

We moved on to the dance floor and soon we were in each other's arms, dancing as close as dignity allowed. I was sure I'd never been as happy as this in all my life up until now. When Greg moved his face nearer mine, I did the most natural thing in the world. I raised my mouth to his and, sliding closer so that our arms were wrapped tightly round each other, we kissed.

"I could do with a bit more of that," he said.

"Me too," I agreed. We kissed again.

We smooched like this for ages, neither of us wanting to be the first to let the other go. And then I felt a tap on my shoulder. I opened one eye lazily and there was Kelly, arms crossed, foot tapping, her mouth in a thin line. Oops!

"The car's waiting for us," she said, pointedly.

"God, Kelly, I'm so-o sorry," I said. "I didn't know it was that late."

Greg, who'd been nuzzling my neck, shifted position and raised his head from my shoulder. "Ah, the lovely Kelly," he said. "Young Chloe here has been on the lookout for you all evening."

"Yeah – right," Kelly muttered. She was looking at me like she wanted to kill me.

"Greg. Kelly. Kelly. Greg," I muttered, feeling really stupid.

"Yeah, I think I know who he is," Kelly said, sarcastically. "Like I said, the car's waiting."

I wanted to stay inside the magic bubble Greg and I had created around ourselves but thanks to Kelly, the spell had been well and truly broken. For tonight at least, the bubble had burst.

I edged away from him. "Greg, I've really got to go."

"Or you'll turn into a pumpkin?"

"Something like that."

"Here." In a repetition of the last occasion, he took my hand and wrote his number. Kelly looked on, her silent fury bouncing off her and on to me.

Only Greg seemed not to feel the atmosphere. "Now, give me yours," he said.

I scribbled my number on his shirtsleeve, at his insistence. He was too hairy to be written on, he said. "Promise me you won't wash until you've transferred it to your address book," he added.

"I promise," I said. Then, blowing him a final kiss, I reluctantly trailed off to join Kelly.

chapter seventeen

Outside Kelly really let rip.

"You've got a bloody nerve, I'll give you that, Chloe Dove," she yelled. "Dragging me all this way just to dump me in a roomful of strangers. Did it ever occur to you I might appreciate being introduced to one or two people?"

"Kelly, I said I was sorry," I pleaded. "I've behaved really badly. I'm really, really sorry."

It made no difference. She was still looking at me coldly. I tried to explain about Greg. How I'd wondered if I'd ever see him again. How I'd never met anyone like him before. Hadn't she ever felt like that about a boy? I asked her.

"I'd never leave you on your own and just go off

with him even if I had," she said.

This was a joke. I'd lost count of the number of times she'd done exactly that. But still. I was in the wrong. I made one last effort to apologize but Kelly simply turned away. So I tried wheedling.

"Aw, come on, Kelly," I pleaded. "There were plenty of other guys around. Couldn't you have got off with one of them?" I asked her.

She sneered at me. "Don't think I didn't try," she said. "Only I wasn't A-list enough to get near. It may have escaped your notice but the place was crawling with minders. They had a list of names. Mine wasn't on it. Clearly I'm not good enough for your new pals." She rounded on me with a jabbing finger. "Tell you what, Chloe, I've always thought this about you. You're a snob. And tonight you've proved it. You couldn't even spare ten minutes to introduce me to your new friends."

Something snapped inside me. Everything I'd ever felt and wanted to say about Kelly suddenly surfaced. I knew there'd be no going back after this, but that was fine by me.

"And you know what, you're just jealous!" I yelled back. "You just can't cope with the fact that it was me who was the centre of attention for once and not you."

"Jealous! Me, jealous of you? You must be joking," she spluttered.

"How have things turned out like this, eh, Kelly? Me up there on the screen and you watching?"

Kelly flinched but I was determined to have my say. "Shouldn't it be the other way round? Isn't that what you're thinking? You've been sulking about me becoming a model ever since the day I was spotted. At least you're honest about it, I suppose."

"Which is more than you are! Why didn't you tell me you were coming here as part of the floor show? I thought we'd be together having a laugh all night."

"I didn't tell you because I knew you'd accuse me of showing off if I did." I paused to draw breath.

"Which is what you've been doing from the start," she fumed. "ME, ME, ME! That's all we ever hear about these days. MY portfolio, MY new way with make-up, MY last modelling job."

"And why shouldn't I talk about what I've done once in a while? Why is everything a competition with you? Why are you so determined to PUNISH me just because for once in my life I've achieved something?"

"PUNISH you? What do you mean PUNISH you?"

"All that stuff with the holiday, making other arrangements without discussing it with me first. How do you think that made me feel?"

"I don't care how it made you feel," Kelly snapped. "Why should I? How do you think I feel when everybody turns round and stares at you at college because you're a model? What am I supposed to do when that happens?"

Well, if that wasn't an admission of jealousy, then I was a banana.

"What are you supposed to do?" I yelled. "You just get on with it, Kelly. Like I've had to every time you make your mind up to go after the thing I want. If it's trainers I couldn't afford then you'd be running off to Daddy to get the money for them so you could get them before I'd managed to save up even half what they cost. If it's anything else, stuff that money can't buy, like exam success or being spotted in the Mall, then you just talk it down so much I end up feeling it's not even worth having."

"Don't talk soft," she said. "As if I've ever been so small-minded."

The driver of the car, who'd been leaning on the bonnet waiting for us when we'd come out, decided he'd heard enough and retreated back into the warmth of the driver's seat. I couldn't say I blamed him. This was no place for the faint-hearted. But I, for one, hadn't finished yet.

"I'll tell you just how small-minded you can be," I said. "Not once have you ever said congratulations to me. Either for this video, or for being spotted in the first place. After all the times I've supported you in your dance competitions and your drama competitions. All those times I've sat boosting your ego whenever you've been for auditions you didn't think you'd get."

I opened the door of the front passenger seat. If I sat in the back with Kelly, one of us would have killed the other before the journey ended, for sure. The driver leaned across to open the door for her. She slid into her seat, a real feat considering how tight her dress was, but not before she shoved her face in at my window and yelled, "Just remember one thing, Chloe. If it hadn't been for me you'd never have gone to that Fashion Show in the first place. You'd have stayed in all afternoon with your head in your books as usual. Now, where was the thanks for that, eh?"

I flopped back on to the seat, suddenly exhausted. This was not how I wanted to remember this night. *Let her have the last word*, I told myself. Kelly and I were finished. There was no point even trying to keep up appearances from now on.

chapter eighteen

I fell into bed exhausted. The next thing I knew someone was hammering on my door.

"You've left your new phone on the kitchen table and it's ringing, Chloe. Shall I answer it?" It was Lindsay.

I groaned a few incomprehensible expletives — at least I hope they were incomprehensible in case Mum and Dad were anywhere in the vicinity — but she wouldn't stop hammering on the door.

"It's someone called Greg."

I practically fell out of bed and lunged across the room to the door.

"Why didn't you tell me? Oh, shut up." There was no time to listen to Lindsay's protestations that in fact she'd been trying to get me to wake up for the last five minutes. I reached the phone in ten seconds flat.

"Greg?"

"Were you expecting someone else? I hope I'm not a disappointment." His low, seductive voice rolled over me in the way I remembered from last night.

"I thought you'd be in bed still."

"No rest for the wicked. Although I wish you'd stayed with me last night. We could have been wicked together."

"What are you ringing me for, Greg?" My steeliness was an act. Inside my guts were in a double knot.

"I want you to give me your address. I have a morning to myself before my world changes for ever."

"That sounds a bit dramatic."

"Believe me, Chloe, it's the truth. We're off on this promo tour later today. From Aberdeen to — do you know any towns beginning with Z?"

I confessed I didn't, unless you counted Zagreb.

"Whatever," he went on. "The video's on TV later today. Everyone will know my face. I'll no longer be a free man. Who better to spend my last hours of liberty with than the girl with the melancholy eyes that I seem to have fallen in love with?"

"Who's that then?" I joked.

"Come on, Chloe. Give me the directions, quick. I love talking to you on the phone, but I'd prefer you in the flesh. So to speak."

I got a glimpse of myself in the kitchen mirror. How rough did I look?

"Er, no, Greg. Actually I don't think that's a good idea."

It would take most of the morning – what was left of it – to make me anywhere near presentable. What was I supposed to wear for one thing? Then there was the house and my parents, not to mention Lindsay! He wouldn't believe me if I said she was my personal assistant. Help! There just wasn't time to get my embarrassing family out of the country and hire Laurence Llewellyn-Bowen in to make over the house!

"Come on, Chloe. Don't be a spoilsport. I'm ready to leave."

Me too, I almost said. If he saw me in these suburban surroundings he would go right off me. I tried again.

"Don't you think you'd be better off resting while you still can?" I said. "I mean, once you're on the road you'll have no chance."

But he wasn't having any, and in the end, short of putting him off so much he'd think I never wanted to see him ever again, I had no choice but to give him directions.

"I'll see you in an hour," he said, and hung up.

Mum, Dad and Lindsay were in the living room, surrounded by a sea of Sunday papers and empty mugs of tea. The place was the usual bomb-site it was at weekends. I took a deep breath to try to calm myself down, but it had no effect on my rising hysteria.

"Mum, Dad!" I squawked, flapping my arms about like a maniac. "You've got to help me. Greg Geffen will be here in an hour. This place looks like a bomb's hit it! Do something, everybody."

Lindsay's mouth dropped to the floor. "Greg Geffen here?" she squeaked. I nodded, as I dashed round the room sweeping up everything that lay in my path.

Mum was knitting her brow. She clearly had no idea who I was talking about, but as soon as I reminded her that he was one of the singers in the boy-band she jumped into action and tried to galvanize Dad into joining her. Not that it did much good.

"I'm staying put," he said, stubbornly. "I'm not changing my routine for Greg bloody Geffen or for any bloody boy-band. It'd take the entire line-up of Jefferson Airplane for me to get off this couch on a Sunday morning and since it's not likely they'll ever show up in these parts then you can forget it."

"Who?" I mouthed over his head at Mum.

"Never mind, there isn't time," she yelled, impatiently. "Now, just go and get a shower and make yourself presentable. You can't open the door looking like that."

I mumbled a grateful thank you and skipped off at double speed.

chapter nineteen

Lindsay and I held our breath and tracked Greg's progress as he switched off the engine, flung open the door of his low-slung red sports car, swung his gorgeous legs round on to the pavement and followed with the rest of him. Once on the pavement he scratched his head, pulled his leather jacket around him to keep out the cold and peered up and down the street. I ran out to meet him.

A slow, appreciative smile spread across his face. "Chloe!" he said. "You look great."

With some of the money I'd earned from the video I'd treated myself to a pair of black leather trousers — something I'd always coveted. This was their first outing. I'd paired them with a cream silk sweater I'd bid a fiver for after the catalogue job, because it had been kicked about a bit and none of the other girls wanted it. To complete the ensemble I'd slung the leather sheepskin flying jacket I'd picked up for a song at the local market around my shoulders to ward off the cold. Lindsay's eyes had boggled when she'd seen me and commented how different I looked. Praise indeed, coming from her. More importantly, if Greg had said it too, it must be true.

There was a shuffle behind me. Lindsay was at the door.

"Come in quick. They're showing the video on T4 after the break."

Lindsay's words spurred Greg into action. He strode down our drive like it was his own, calling out over his shoulder that we'd miss it if we didn't hurry, while I scuttled behind with geisha-girl meekness.

In the living room my parents feigned relaxed indifference to Greg's appearance, although all traces of mugs, newspapers and crumbs had vanished. Lindsay, by contrast, was as giddy as a spinning top. She quivered in front of the TV, remote aimed at the screen, ready to turn up the volume once the adverts finished.

"Greg Geffen in our living room. I can't believe it!" she squealed.

Greg acknowledged her homage with a modest smile and said hello to everyone. Mum gave a nervous cough and Dad rolled his eyes in middle-class embarrassment. The first boy I bring home and he has to be a rock star, I could practically hear him thinking. There was some more awkward silence while we all sat down again, then thankfully, the ads were over and it was back to the show and straight into the video.

As the video progressed, Greg started to relax, and at the point where he and I appeared together for the first time – to huge family applause – he took my hand, squeezed it and gave me a broad wink. I blushed like mad, pleased, but unable to look at him with my family staring at us like that.

When it finished Lindsay leaped up and started hopping around saying things like "just wait till my friends start ringing me up", for all the world as if she'd been in the video herself. She went on like that for ages until even Greg must have got sick of hearing how fantastic he was and Mum finally put an end to the floor show.

"Lindsay, I need you to help me with the lunch," she said. "Will you be staying, Greg? You're very welcome."

Please say no, I prayed. It flashed into my mind that Greg didn't belong here. He wasn't part of this life, in this house, and that was fine with me. There would be another kind of life with Greg, and it wouldn't involve sitting round the dining-room table eating Sunday roast, with my dad quizzing him about his education and my mum interrogating him over his political views.

"You can have my roasties," Lindsay said. "My diet starts today. I mean properly this time."

"Maybe another time," he said. "This is only a flying visit."

"Well, you'll always be welcome," Mum said, but I wasn't convinced she meant it. She ushered the other two out. Dad was clearly relieved that he wasn't expected to make small talk, but Lindsay was full of mutinous mutterings that weren't quelled until Greg promised to send her a signed picture of the band and a signed copy of the single, plus the album, too, as soon as it was released.

Finally we were alone. "I thought they'd never take the hint," he said.

He dropped his hands on my shoulders for a moment while he studied me, then began to trace the outline of my face with rapt concentration. I was practically melting with lust. But this was the living room at one o'clock on a Sunday afternoon. I could hear the pots and pans rattling in the kitchen, the familiar voices of my parents muted in conversation. Any minute now, Lindsay could storm the room. She was probably outside already, peering through the keyhole.

"God, Chloe," he said. "I can't tell you how much I've been thinking about you since the first time we met. Last night, well, it was a dream come true."

"You could have got in touch sooner, you know," I rebuked him. "The agency has my number."

He shook his head. "I know," he said. "Sounds so simple, doesn't it? But, you see, when you didn't contact me . . . well, I thought it was because you didn't want to see me again."

"Well, I did," I said. "And I do."

Then we slid our arms around each other and kissed long and deep. I resisted the urge to allow Greg to manoeuvre me back on to the settee, although it was what I wanted more than anything.

Fortunately for both of us, his mobile went off at precisely the moment he was sliding his hand beneath my top.

"Shit. I'd better get that. It's probably Buzz."

He scrabbled for his phone, swearing under his breath as he dug around in his pocket. While he talked I took the opportunity to rearrange my hair as I listened in. He was leaving right now, he said, and would be back well before three o'clock.

"But you've only just got here," I said.

"I'm sorry, babe. But Buzz insists," he sighed.

Bang on cue, her disembodied head sticking round the door like a coconut on a shy, Lindsay appeared. "Can I come and see you out, too?" she asked.

Behind Greg's head I mouthed, "Get lost!"

Greg was more polite. "See, Linds, I'm not – um – sure when I'll – um – get the chance. . ."

"OK, OK, I get the message." She flounced out.

"BUT I'LL SEND YOU A POSTCARD!" This to her retreating back.

There was a faint reply. "Oh, dear, have I offended her?" he asked. "Can't have her spreading it around that I'm rude to my fans."

"It'll take more than that," I reassured him.

At the car, he took my hand and kissed it gently.

"I promise you I'll text you or call you from every town we visit," he said. "If I can talk to you every day then I'll keep sane."

Then he was gone. I watched the car until there was nothing to see and only a distant roar of the engine reminded me he had ever been here in the first place. I trailed back up the drive into the house and closed the door behind me, half wondering if any of his new-found fame would rub off on me, and what it would be like.

chapter twenty

That afternoon the madness began. The phone never stopped ringing, although in the beginning it wasn't for me. Lindsay's little cronies from school were clearly as big fans of Tough Love as she was herself. She must have been showing off on my behalf for weeks now about me being in the video – which came as a huge surprise to me since she'd never been one to blow my trumpet. In fact I felt like this was the first time she'd ever as much as acknowledged my existence – although of course that worked both ways.

Anyway the little chums hogged the phone for most of the afternoon as one by one they rang to quiz her about my part in the video, and to ask if she could get the band's autographs. Clearly in her element, Lindsay described Greg's visit and how she'd sat next to him on the settee and chatted to him for absolutely hours. I listened in, leaning up against the kitchen door, my mouth dropping open further with each new embellishment.

"He promised to send me a postcard from every town he visits," she bragged to one particular caller. "I'll let you have a read if you like, but I wouldn't want to keep pestering him for autographs. You know how it is."

"Tracey Butterworth," she said, after she'd put the phone down on that particular one. She rubbed her hands with glee. "I am SO not going to give her an autograph."

"Oh?"

"She thinks I've forgotten how she dobbed on me to Miss Newcombe for copying her French. Well, she can think again. I'll let Meg Carter have it instead. It's her birthday soon, and she says her dad says she can have a proper disco. She's never invited me before, but she will now."

Her eyes gleamed in triumph.

"Lindsay, you can't barter Greg's autographs just to get even with the people you don't like, or to curry favour with those people who don't like you."

"Can't I? Just watch me." She snatched the phone up as it rang again. This time it was for me.

It was the local paper. And they wanted to interview me.

"Me?" I squeaked. "What do you want to interview me for?"

They were taking the mickey, surely. Or was it Kelly, looking for some sweet revenge by getting one of her acting mates to ring my house and pretend to be from the press?

"Well, you know. About modelling."

"I don't know anything about modelling," I said. "Well, a bit, but not enough to fill up an interview. I've only done two jobs so far."

"Now don't be modest, Chloe. You're a bit of a celebrity now, you know. Just say yes."

"How did you get my number?" I wanted to know.

"Your agency rang us. Serena Montague?"

"I'll have to check first," I said, as snootily as I could manage. There was no way I was going to fall for this one if it turned out to be Kelly after all.

"That's up to you," the voice on the other end said. "I'll leave my name and number, then when you're ready you can get back to me."

In a daze I put the phone down. What had that woman said? That I was a bit of a celebrity? Well, I guess if the number of phone calls to our house this afternoon was anything to go by then she was right. Maybe I owed it to my public not to be a recluse.

The phone continued to ring for Lindsay all afternoon. Mum and Dad sloped off for a walk, leaving Lindsay and me to do the dishes. That done, I resolved to crawl off to my bed. I was knackered. But no sooner had I put my head on the pillow, than it started again. I charged out of my room and reached the phone moments before Lindsay. If this was another one of Lindsay's mates they were going to get an ear bashing from me.

"Chloe Dove," I snapped.

"Strewth. Have I got you at a bad time? Should I ring back?"

"Er. Do I know you?" I'd been on TV for all of three minutes forty seconds and already I was behaving like a diva. Actually, even as I asked the question I realized that I only knew one person with an accent like that.

"It's Rob. Rob McGrath, you know, from. . ."

"Sorry, sorry, sorry. Of course. It's just — the

phone hasn't stopped ringing all afternoon."

Mortified with embarrassment about how rude I must have sounded, I prattled on for ages about my sister's friends hogging the phone while wishing he'd shut me up. Why had he rung? I wondered. When I finally ran out of amusing anecdotes, he told me.

"Yeah, well, it was the vid I was calling about, actually. I just wanted to say congrats."

"Oh. Cheers."

"Shame about the song, though."

"Don't you like it?"

"Shit, no. D'you?" He asked like it went without saying. Actually, up until now I'd not given it much thought. I was interested in the singer, not the song.

"You hate boy-bands," he said.

"Do I? How do you know?"

"I remember you saying so when Uncle Charlie was taking your photos."

"Er, well. I suppose there's boy-bands and boy-bands."

You could almost hear the squelch of the sticky silence that was now beginning to ooze down the line.

"Well, thanks for calling, Rob," I said, when it became clear that Rob was in no hurry to speak first. "It was nice of you to remember me."

"Yeah, well. Serena was staying and she gave me your number. She says hi and she'll be ringing you. Something about this being a real break for you."

"Oh, rubbish."

"No, really."

"Not as much of a break as for the band."

"Guess not." A beat, then: "Which one's yours, then?"

"Rob! Am I that transparent?"

"Like a window with no glass in. Go on, then. Which one?"

"The one with the shortest hair who does most of the singing," I said.

I didn't mention the crinkly eyes and the sexy smile that was not a smile, not to mention the long legs and the cute butt.

"Oh, I know. The short one."

"He's not short," I objected.

"Everybody's short as far as I'm concerned."

That was my problem, too, but I wasn't going to sympathize. I was mortally offended that Rob had called my boyfriend short. There was a long pause

I'd no intention of filling after that!

"So, anyway. You're happy then."

I thought about it. It wasn't so simple.

"Well, yes with the video and Greg and everything. But last night turned out to be a bit of a disaster in other ways."

"Oh?"

I fiddled with the phone cord for a bit before saying: "Well, I had a blazing row with my best friend."

"How come?"

I told him about Kelly, and the atmosphere we'd parted in.

"She's probably just a wee bit jealous," he said. "She'll probably come round."

"Yeah, you're right." How could I possibly explain Kelly and me over the phone? Gloom was descending again and this was not good. "Anyway," I joked, "what's with the Scottish?"

"How do you mean?"

I reminded him of what he'd said. "Nobody says 'wee' in England," I said.

"Well, I do — since I spent two weeks there over Christmas. I've fallen in love with the word."

"How can you fall in love with a word?"

Although I understood it, really. I was in love with lots of words. Cedar. Languid. Conspiracy. I could go on.

Robbie seemed suddenly agitated. "Chloe, I have to go now," he said. "My uncle's tapping his watch."

I laughed. "I thought that only happened in our house," I said.

"Nah. My uncle's a miserable skinflint. World-famous for it. Travels in the baggage hold and pockets the money he saves on expenses."

"Should meet my dad."

"That right? OK. I'll get off the line then."

That was twice now. He was so out of order here. It was ME who should have ended the call. I mean, who called who?

"Nice talking to you, Chloe."

"Bye, then."

"Oh, and just one thing before I go."

"Mm?"

"You be careful now."

"Meaning?"

"Meaning just that."

"Well, why wouldn't I be?"

"No reason. Just reminding you, that's all."

The phone went dead.

chapter twenty-one

I don't know what I expected once the video was shown. I didn't exactly become a household name, but people I'd never spoken to at college before started to say hello to me and once on the bus I thought the driver looked at me a bit oddly when I flashed my bus pass.

The paper did its interview and published a couple of ghastly out of focus photos alongside the copy, and one of the secretaries at college laminated it and stuck it up on the wall of fame.

Meanwhile I kept in touch with the agency, who kept offering me jobs I had to turn down because of college commitments. I was willing and able to drop everything for even a sniff of a go-see, but

Serena always talked me out of it.

"Stick with college for one more term, Chloe and then I promise you as much modelling work as you want. You know it makes sense," she told me. Dad, of course, thoroughly approved and I guess it was Serena's practical attitude that won him over to the idea of me modelling in the end.

Coming home from college one afternoon, I dropped into Sainsbury's. Mum was out on the razzle with a bunch of girlfriends and it was Dad's night to teach his evening class. I was in charge of the cooking.

Normally I would have picked up a couple of pizzas and a bag of salad and headed for the check-out, but tonight I dawdled. It was difficult to know what to choose for Lindsay nowadays. She complained if Mum dished up too little on her plate that it was up to her to decide if she needed to eat less, and if she was given too much she complained Mum was trying to make her fatter than she was. Yesterday she'd simply refused to come to the table, which had spoiled lunch completely as far as Mum and I were concerned, because for the duration of the meal we'd been forced to listen to Dad ranting on about starving millions *blah, blah, blah*.

What was going on with her? I wondered, as I picked up ready-prepared meals for two, read the list of contents then replaced them in the chill cabinet.

At the checkout, the woman ahead of me started a conversation, half with me, half with the girl on the till.

"I know I shouldn't, 'cos I'm on a diet," she said. "But I can resist anything except temptation."

I glanced at the stuff she'd bought and realized that absolutely everything she was buying had "fat-free" or "low-sugar" written on it somewhere. Everything, that is, apart from the huge bar of chocolate that she was even now scooping up and shoving furtively into her white plastic carrier bag, as if she expected that any minute she'd be arrested by the Fat Police for exceeding her daily calorie allowance.

I smiled weakly as the woman, having paid her bill, picked up her bags and shuffled off, and took my turn. Fresh pasta, pesto, parmesan cheese, fruit, salad and bread. Oh, and a packet of Penguins and a chocolate cheesecake.

"I can see you don't need to watch your weight," the checkout girl remarked, with a baleful look in her eye. "I only need to look at a chocolate biscuit and I put on two pounds."

I handed over the money and put my hand out for the change, then picked up the two bags I'd managed to fill.

"Oh, don't worry," I said. "I generally make sure I sick it all up within half an hour of scoffing it."

The look of shocked amazement on the girl's face was a joy to behold.

"Only joking," I said, and headed for the exit. That would teach her to stop making personal remarks, I thought, as I snaked my way through the crowds of shoppers.

Back home Lindsay was in the kitchen slicing up an apple into about sixteen wafer-thin segments, her face as long as the M11.

"Any phone calls?" I asked, as she looked up, registered my presence and returned to her task.

"Haven't you got your own phone now you're making pots of money?"

"Well, yes. But. . ."

"But you're that desperate you gave him both numbers, I know."

"What is your problem?" I snarled. "PMS again?"

I slammed the Sainsbury's bags down on the

counter. All I wanted was one lousy phone call. Greg had warned me that it was going to be nigh on impossible for him to have any privacy on their publicity tour for the new single but so far all I'd had was two text messages and that was it. *Stay beautiful, babe*, he'd written on both occasions. Well, not everyone could be Shakespeare, I suppose.

"Anyway, what you doing with that fruit? I wouldn't want you to spoil your appetite for the delicious feast I am about to prepare," I said, with as much sarcasm as I could muster.

I began striding around the kitchen, setting down pans, running water, unwrapping all the stuff I'd bought.

"Oh, don't bother cooking for me," Lindsay said. "I'm absolutely not eating another thing today."

"Lindsay. You must eat something. You'll make yourself ill," I said.

"I've had some fruit and that's my lot," she said stubbornly, "so don't try to make me eat anything else. Anyway, it's nothing to do with you what I eat. You're not my mother."

I opened my mouth to say something when my phone went off, sending me leaping about three feet into the air. It was Greg. If it had been anyone else I would have asked them to ring later, honestly. But come on! Greg, for Chrissake!

I skipped into my room and draped myself fetchingly across the bed, in seductive preparation for his honeyed words.

All I got was a string of moans. He was tired, he had the mother of all headaches, and as soon as he'd eaten he had to spend the rest of the evening signing photos for fans.

Did I have PUNCH BAG tattooed across my forehead today, or something? First Lindsay, now him.

"Tell you what," I snapped. "You do my timed English essay and I'll sign a few autographs."

"I was only saying. It's not easy being a pop star, you know." He sounded hurt and hard done by, which had the effect of irritating me even more. What on earth did he have to whinge about?

"Beats going down a coal mine I should think," I said. "Or sleeping rough."

"If you knew one half of the things I've had to put up with today. . ."

"And if you knew how much college work I've got," I countered.

"For God's sake. I left school at sixteen without a single qualification to my name! College work. I don't know why you're bothering."

Was it possible to leave school with NO qualifications these days, I wondered. Surely Greg could have scraped together one or two GCSE's? They were hardly rocket science, after all.

"I'm bothering because I can't sing," I snapped. "So I'd better have a few qualifications instead."

"You don't need college with your looks," Greg said.

"What?" I moved the phone away from my ear and stared at it in disbelief. Had I heard right? What had looks to do with anything? Had he never heard of women's rights? And did he know the average length of a model's shelf life?

"Chloe. CHLO-EE! Are you there? What have I done? Talk to me!"

"I'm here," I said. Greg sounded frantic. It may have been perverse, but having Greg on the edge of grovelling to me made me feel extremely powerful.

"Are you angry at me? Shall I sing to you?" Down the phone he crooned, "Please forgive me, darling Chloe" to the tune of "Be The One".

"Are we friends now?" he asked me.

"Could be," I muttered. I was enjoying my position far too much to relinquish it so easily.

"You're a hard woman, Chloe Dove," he said. "Do I have to grovel?"

"If you want." I was flirting with him now and from what he said next, I knew he appreciated it.

"God, I wish we could spend some time together," he groaned. "This is no way to go on. I'm sick of this touring lark. The other guys are driving me nuts."

"You're just tired," I soothed. Now was clearly the time to show my sympathetic side. "And you've been living in each other's pockets all this time. You're bound to get fed up with each other."

"Maybe." Greg didn't sound convinced.

"I thought you were all bosom buddies. That's what I read in my kid sister's magazine, anyway. And what about the video? All that hugging and male bonding stuff?"

"Media hype. This is strictly business. Every one of us is in this to get a solo career, though I'm the only one with a good enough voice to do it. Not that I'm showing off or anything."

"No, course not. You've a great voice. No point pretending different."

"Listen, Chloe. I have to go. Some idiot keeps giving me hand signals. I'd give him one back, only it might turn up in tomorrow's paper."

"You mean you've got the press there?"

He sighed. "Right now I can't take a pee in peace," he said. "But if it helps sell records I'll give the bastards exactly what they want. I'll ring again, when I get the chance. Stay beautiful, babe."

I was going to have to stop him using that phrase. Surely a touch of originality couldn't be that difficult for someone who was supposed to have so much input into the band's lyrics?

chapter twenty-two

I was cycling home from college, my face rigid with cold and my hands and feet in the first stages of frostbite, wondering how it was that a pleasant bike ride on a warm summer's evening, which got you home almost before you'd realized you'd arrived, could seem like a month-long trek across the North Pole once winter bit. I was thinking about hot buttered toast and jam when my phone rang. The shock of hearing it go off when I wasn't expecting it almost sent me catapulting over the handlebars, until I managed to right myself at the last second. It was Greg. Since I'd been mean to him on the phone, he'd taken to ringing me more often. Proof that treating 'em mean really did keep 'em keen.

Fortunately, I had already turned into our street. I decided to push the bike the rest of the way and talk to him as I went.

"You're on a bike? A motorbike?"

"As if. Although I am in leathers. Sort of."

I'd become so attached to my flying jacket and leather pants that I rarely wore anything else these days.

"Now that I'd love to see," Greg said, voice dripping with lust.

"Easy, tiger."

It crossed my mind that the next time I met up with Greg I'd find it a lot more difficult to fend him off in person than I did over the phone — always assuming I wanted to, of course, and that was becoming less and less clear to me the more I got to know him.

"Don't tell me you're on a push bike?"

"What's so bad about that? I'm doing my bit for the environment. Anyway, we're not all earning pots of money."

"If only," Greg sighed. "I haven't seen any money yet — apart from the miserable weekly allowance we get given."

"That right? Good job I only want you for your

body, then."

I'd intended what I'd said just as a joke – an example of my witty repartee. It had never been my intention to broach the subject of sex. Or maybe it had. The unconscious, after all, is a strange and powerful thing. But raising the topic – by whatever means – had made me jittery, setting me off gabbling at length about My Day So Far, in an attempt to sidetrack him.

"Chloe. Listen, I'm in a hurry," he interrupted.

So, I wasn't the only one who found my life boring, then?

"This weekend. I have an invite to a great party. Exclusive. If you came down for it, well, you could stay on afterwards."

I was turning into the drive now, and came to a standstill at his words. A light appeared suddenly in the hallway and the doorway opened up a crack. Dad.

"Chloe! Is that you? What are you doing hovering in the drive like that? Are you coming in or not?"

"Chloe. Tell me you'll come and stay. I promise you you won't regret it."

His voice was no more than a breath.

"It's not that easy," I hedged. "There's my mum and dad."

There were other considerations too – not least where I would be expected to sleep. It was clear what Greg expected, but then he didn't know about my virginal state.

"Oh, come on. Don't you want to be with me just as much as I want to be with you?"

"CHLOE! ARE YOU ON THAT PHONE? FOR GOODNESS' SAKE HANG UP AND COME IN! THERE'S A DRAUGHT."

"Course I do, Greg. But you must have heard that? My dad. What am I supposed to say to him?"

"Tell him some lies. Fucksake. People lie all the time."

I thought about that one. Did they? I needed more time. I so wanted to see Greg again, but was I ready for the next step?

"Listen. I'll work something out. It's Monday now. I'll ring you on Friday. With a plan."

"I need something more certain than a plan," Greg groaned.

"A plan will have to do," I said in a stage whisper. If my dad hadn't been suspicious before he stuck his head outside, he surely must be now.

"Goodnight, Greg. Speak to you soon."

"You're driving me wild, Chloe."

"Am I?"

"You know it. Stay beautiful, babe."

"CHLOE."

"I'm coming, aren't I? Just let me put my bike away."

In the living room Lindsay sat huddled in one corner of the settee. She looked like she'd been crying.

"What's up?" I asked, in a mild attempt to be sisterly.

"Nothing," she snapped. "Go away."

"Fine," I said. "Don't say I didn't want to know."

I trailed into the kitchen.

"What's the matter with her?" I asked Mum, who was sitting at the kitchen table beneath a mound of paperwork.

When she raised her eyes from the file she was reading, looking thoroughly harassed, I took the decision that it was probably better not to mention the fact that I couldn't smell dinner cooking, in case I got my head bitten off.

"Oh, she's just upset, that's all. Somebody said something to her. You know what these girls are like."

"Said what?" I was curious.

"Oh, I don't know. Something about how unlikely it was that she'd ever get the chance to be a model like her sister, with the figure she has. Honestly, girls can be so cruel."

I could feel my lips twitch, but had the grace to cover my mouth.

"Well, she's hardly one for diplomacy herself, is she?" I said. "When Kelly came with me to the launch party, Lindsay told her she looked like she'd been Tangoed."

"She didn't!"

"Oh, yes she did. Mind you, she was right."

"What's happened to Kelly?" Mum said. "She's not shown her face round here for ages."

"No, and she's not likely to," I said. "Let's say we've parted ways."

Mum was reading again. "Oh, well," she said. "These things happen. Are you bothered?"

I realized that I'd barely given Kelly a thought in weeks.

"Actually, I don't think I am," I said.

"Good." I couldn't help picking up relief in Mum's voice. Clearly, she was too busy for a heart to heart. Perhaps now was not the time to approach her about my approaching date with Greg.

"Look, love. Do me a favour, will you? Go and have a word with Lindsay. Be nice to her. If I don't get this read before the staff meeting tomorrow I've had it. And I've not even started on supper yet."

Bloody hell! She wanted *me* to be nice to Lindsay! She was clearly overworked.

In the living room Lindsay still hadn't shifted position.

"I don't know about you but I'm starving," I said. "Fancy some toast? There's no sign of supper."

Lindsay drew her mouth into a thin line. "I'm on a diet. Remember?"

"Aw, come on, Lindsay," I pleaded. "You shouldn't take any notice of what ignorant people say. A bit of toast won't kill you."

"I said no and I mean no," she yelled. "If I eat one piece of toast then I'll end up eating my way through an entire loaf, just like I always end up doing. I'm better off not eating anything at all."

I hovered above her, trying to make sense of her twisted logic. I'd read about binge eating in magazines. Is that what Lindsay was doing?

Bingeing and putting on weight, then punishing herself by denying herself food afterwards?

"Lindsay," I wanted to know. "When did you last eat?"

"None of your business. I'm going up for a bath."

Dad popped his round the living-room door as she scrambled to her feet. "Everything all right in here, you two?" he asked.

We both nodded, but it must have been clear it wasn't. Lindsay walked right past without looking at either of us.

I stared after her, wishing Dad hadn't come in right at that moment. I could have talked to her. What was I supposed to do now? Tell Mum and let her sort it out? Say nothing at all and wait for Lindsay to come to her senses?

chapter twenty-three

Lindsay's problems were dwarfed by pressing questions of my own that I still didn't have answers to. Where was I going to stay in London and how was I going to explain the weekend away to my parents? I imagined Tough Love fans all over England wishing they had my problem. I imagined Kelly in my ear saying, *What's the big deal? It's about time you lost your cherry.* I'd always maintained that when I did lose my virginity it would be through choice, and not because I had no alternative. If I stayed at Greg's place then he would assume I was up for it. I had to have a Plan B, just in case I bottled it at the last minute.

Who did I know in London? Suddenly, I had a

road to Damascus moment. Of course! It was obvious! Why had it taken me so long to think of Sofia?

She seemed overjoyed to hear from me and wouldn't even let me get to the end of my stammering request before issuing an invitation.

"So, who will you be going to this *exclusive* party with?" There was a teasing note to her voice. "Anyone I know?"

Shyly, I admitted it was Greg.

"So why aren't you staying with him, then? Not that it's any of my business."

"Well. . ."

"Forgive me, Chloe, that was very rude of me. My mother always told me not to ask personal questions, but I never learn."

It was impossible to take offence at anything Sofia said. She was just, so, well – nice, I guess.

"Actually, I think we may be going to the same party. Don't be taken in by the word 'exclusive', though! I think you'll find it's just PR speak. There'll probably just be loads of people there from Big Brother and Pop Idol if my experience of these bashes is anything to go by. But there'll be masses of champagne, so usually that makes up for the disappointment of not seeing anyone on the A-list."

I clearly had a lot to learn about the party circuit, but at least I wasn't alone. Greg, it seemed, was also about to find himself on a steep learning curve.

"Anyway, just take a taxi from the station and arrive any time. Not before midday, though. Just in case. I've been working non-stop this week and I need my beauty sleep."

Clearly her modelling career was much more successful than mine.

"And you?" she wanted to know. "Done much since the video?"

I mentioned my foray into the glamorous world of catalogue modelling. Sofia sympathized.

"But actually, I've got A levels coming up soon. I promised Serena I'd devote this time to my books. Gets my dad off my back too. Next year, though, I intend to make some serious money." I tried to sound confident and go-getting.

"It'll be so good to talk to someone normal at the weekend," she said. "Honestly, that pair I'm sharing with are driving me nuts."

"How come?"

It was hard to imagine sunny-natured Sofia brought low by other people. Although I didn't know her well, so far she'd given me the clear impression that she was impervious to the complicated moods of others.

"Oh, the usual drama," she said. "Tillie seems to have developed a major dose of schizophrenia, full of the joys one moment, everybody's best friend, deliriously happy – you know the kind of thing. Next day she won't get out of bed unless Kendall stands over her and threatens what she'll do to her unless she does. God, the rows they have."

"You don't think – I mean – I wouldn't want to make things more awkward. . . Kendall's scary enough at the best of times."

"Nonsense. Kendall's a pussy cat."

"Yeah, pussy cats have claws and teeth, remember. I hardly know her but she always makes me feel I did something to upset her."

"Oh, Kendall's like that with everyone," Sofia reassured me. "It's all part of her image. She likes to think she's one of the common people. Although it doesn't stop her drinking champagne and going out to dinner with rich men."

Sofia was sharper than she liked to let on, clearly.

"Anyway, it's official – you're coming. Besides, I want to show you my new Manolos."

"Oh, well. In that case, I can hardly refuse, can I?" I said, hoping the fact that I hadn't a clue what she was talking about was undetectable.

My next phone call wasn't so pleasant. Whenever I've got something unpleasant to say to someone, I dither over my words longer than Posh Spice must spend choosing which shoes to put on in the morning. I had rehearsed a good opening line, and decided that as long as I kept on-message, Greg wouldn't be able to deflect me from my purpose.

"What d'you want first? The good news, or the bad?"

"Aw, Chloe. Come on. Are you coming to London or not? Stop messing me about."

"Good news or bad? Choose."

Greg sighed long and hard. "OK. I'm too knackered to argue with you. The good, please."

"Well, I'm coming."

A beat and then: "There's definitely a but in there, am I right?"

Another beat, then: "Why won't you stay with me, Chloe?" Greg pleaded. "We don't have to sleep in the same bed, if that's what's on your mind. I could sleep on the sofa."

"And my granny can dance the fandango whilst juggling three balls in the air," I said. "Look, Greg. I'm not saying that I'm not ever going to come and stay with you. But, well. I hardly know you, do I? You have to respect the way I feel about this stuff, otherwise we might as well pack it in right now."

"No! For God's sake, Chloe. That's not what I want at all."

"It's not what I want either." His emotional outburst made me almost glow with happiness. So this was what it was like to have a man eating out of your hand. And not just any man, either.

"We can still have a lovely time at the party," he said. "We'll be the best-looking couple there."

"Honestly, Greg, you do say the funniest things."

"Do I?"

"You do indeed. Listen, I've got to go. Let me give you the address where I'll be staying. Have you got a pen?"

I read it out slowly.

"So. You're staying with Tillie and that lot." He was starting to sound tetchy again.

"I'm actually staying as a guest of Sofia's. I don't suppose I'll see the others."

How did he know the address? I wondered. I remembered the black look Kendall had given me at the launch party and the way Tillie had suddenly melted away as soon as Greg had appeared on the scene that night. There was a history between those three, that was for sure. When was I going to find out what it was?

"It's not a problem, is it?" My question came out as the timid squeak of a pathetic mouse.

Greg's reply was brusque. "Sofia's fine, I guess," he said. "It's just those other two. Just take my advice and keep well away from them – poisonous witches."

There was a sharpness in Greg's voice that warned me not to go there. I would keep quiet for now. But that wasn't the end of it.

chapter twenty-four

So here I was in London, on a Saturday afternoon, rummaging through the contents of my weekend bag. I despaired. Glamorous? For a bag lady, possibly. Clearly, I must have been mad to think that either of the two outfits I'd finally packed after an entire morning of feverish indecision could possibly pass muster for anything other than karaoke night at the Rat and Parrot. There was a knock on my bedroom door, and, without waiting for permission to enter, Kendall's white-blonde head appeared. How could anyone look so sultry in faded jeans and a black sweater?

"Thought I'd say hello. Welcome you to the Big Smoke. Can I come in?"

Who was I to say no, especially when she already *was* in? She was eyeing my stuff, clearly under-whelmed. I couldn't blame her, but did she have to make it so obvious?

"That what you're wearing tonight?"

I muttered something non-committal. Kendall probably wore Versace to pop out to the shops.

"Come into my room. I've got a wardrobe full of gear I never wear."

I'd have loved to have been able to turn down the offer, but I'm afraid the thought never entered my head. Tonight was the most important night in my life so far and I *had* to look my best. Which is why I found myself saying: "Well, I don't suppose there's any harm in looking," as I followed her into her room.

Kendall's wardrobe took up most of one wall, in a room bereft of anything much else other than a bed. Clearly, she preferred to put her money on her back rather than invest it in fixtures and fittings.

"Something rock-chick, I think, while it's Greg, waddya reckon?"

"How do you know I'm going with him?"

The edge in my voice must have been sharper than I'd intended.

"Sorr-y," Kendall came back, widening her

turquoise eyes in what was clearly mock apology. "Didn't think it was a secret. It was just something Sofia let slip when she said we was expecting a weekend guest."

She was selecting dresses, tops, skimpy skirts, holding them up for my inspection, then making three piles – yes, no, and maybe, based on some criteria of her own, because I wasn't contributing to the decision-making process in any way whatsoever.

"So, you and Greg not shagging yet, then?"

I must have turned scarlet with embarrassment because Kendall suddenly let out a huge gale of laughter.

"If you could just see your face. You don't have to answer that one anyway, 'cos it's none of my bloody business, I'm just a nosy cow. Now. What do you think of this?"

Triumphantly, she held up a wisp of a dress. It was a rich purple, spattered with beading so that it glinted bewitchingly whenever Kendall turned it this way and that for my inspection.

"Joseph," she said. "Although you can probably tell that."

I couldn't. The only Joseph I knew in the fashion

business was Jo Dickens who ran Cheap Chic, the market stall at home.

Kendall was practically inside the wardrobe now, muttering something about shoes, swept up on an incessant stream of obscenities as she tossed first one pair then another over her shoulder.

"Where the fuck? Ah! Here they are. Perfect, I'm sure you'll agree. All we need now is the bag and the jewellery and then. . ."

Why was Kendall being so nice to me, I wondered. *Keep away from her*, Greg had said, but he wouldn't say why.

I told myself not to be so melodramatic, but I couldn't help the feeling of panic that hit me when I looked down at the outfit Kendall had assembled so neatly on the bed. On either side of the pillow, she'd placed two gold hooped earrings, each with a winking, purple stone hanging from it. Lower down, at neck level, a matching choker, set with the exact same stone, and then the dress — a sliver of silk; diaphanous, purple perfection that I ached to reach out and touch. Where my feet would be, she'd placed a pair of pointed, high-heeled, backless satin shoes, milky-white in colour, and embossed with a purple flower and beading at the toe.

"Looks a bit spooky laid out like that, doesn't it?" she said. "Like some human sacrifice or something."

I didn't want her to see that that was exactly what I'd thought, too.

"You're being very generous," I gushed instead, in an attempt to show her that whatever mind games she was playing didn't even come close to touching me.

Of course, it would have worked better if I'd actually turned it all down in the end. I wanted to say no, I really did, but the truth was, I'd fallen madly in love with the whole outfit. I couldn't possibly wear anything else. I owed it to myself, though, to make one final bid for level pegging with Kendall in the Mean Bitch stakes.

"Don't you think it looks a bit – well, you know, tarty?" I asked her, fingering the material of the dress with just a hint of distaste on my face.

Kendall narrowed her eyes. Good, I'd got her rattled.

"Greg'll be in seventh heaven when he clocks you wearing this lot. He'll probably propose," she said. "He's good at that."

I should have known I'd never be able to get one

over on Kendall. Perhaps I shouldn't even have bothered trying. Next to her I was a rank amateur. I reckon she'd have seen even Kelly off in a bitch fight.

"So what is it with you and Greg? There, I've finally asked you. Now you can stop pretending that you asked me in here to look at clothes," I said, not caring how rattled I appeared any more.

She was putting away the rejected outfits now, slowly, nonchalantly, as if she were building herself up to saying something really important. In a million years I'd never have predicted her next words.

"I hate him," she said. "He uses people. He used Tillie and he'll use you if you let him. He's on the way up and he wants a girlfriend who suits his image. For the moment you're it. Knowing Greg, he'll have had you checked out. Asked Gavin about you. Found out you'd no form but plenty of prospects."

"Gavin?"

"You know. Directed the video. Gavin's a talent-spotter. He did nothing but sing your praises round the water cooler. Said if he wasn't much mistaken you'd be on the cover of *Vogue* this time next year.

That would've registered with Greg."

Briefly, I was diverted by the thought of Gavin's prediction.

"Did he really say that?" I asked.

"*I* don't tell lies," Kendall said, clearly implying that she knew someone who did.

"You'd better get to the point," I said.

"Like I said. Tillie was the one before you. Only she made the mistake of getting pregnant."

I flinched.

"She thought Greg would be delighted. After all, they were engaged to be married. This just kind of brought things forward a bit."

I was beginning to feel sick. Engaged? Pregnant? Of all the things I'd imagined, neither of these had crossed my mind.

"I – I didn't know any of this," I stammered. "I thought maybe you and Greg – from the black looks I saw you give him."

"ME and Greg?" Kendall sneered. "DO me a favour. Although he did try."

God, it got worse.

"So, what happened when she told him she was pregnant?"

"Three guesses," Kendall said, grimly. "He

insisted she got rid of it. So she did."

Somewhere in the middle of Kendall's story I must have taken her silk dress on to my lap. Now I found myself gripping it in both fists, like it was the security blanket I'd had as a child. Was any of this true? Surely not. But why would Kendall tell me all this stuff unless there was at least some truth in it? She must know I'd be unable to keep it to myself. I'd have to tell Greg everything I'd heard. But where would I start? *By the way, Greg, I heard you forced your ex to have an abortion.* How on earth was I supposed to act normal with him when I saw him in less than three hours' time?

"I can see you've had a shock," Kendall said. "Greg'll call me all the names under the sun for this, but I can live with that."

"So, why did you tell me?" I breathed. I hope my question implied that I thought her reasons were as far from noble as a person's could be.

"Because Greg won't, unless you bring it up first, and maybe I think you've got a right to know just what kind of a guy you're involved with," she said.

Then she left me alone to think about what I should do about it.

chapter twenty-five

The news I'd just heard turned on its head everything I thought I knew about Greg. Almost immediately something like a scab began to form over the secret hiding-place in which my feelings about him were locked, protecting my wound at least for now, making it just possible to cope through the hours until I saw Greg again.

I went through the motions of getting ready, but I could salvage no pleasure from it – even when the reflection thrown back at me in the mirror showed a glamorous, elegant young woman, clearly used to stepping out in style. I may have looked like I was Born To Do It, but I sure as hell didn't feel like it as I climbed into the shiny black limo and took my place in the back seat next to Greg.

He leaned over and kissed me, but at the last possible second I moved my head slightly so that his lips landed somewhere on my ear.

"Wow," he breathed. "You look great and you smell even better."

I accepted the compliment as being nothing short of my due. He was right. I did and I did, but so what? I was a model, wasn't I? And he was well used to having beautiful women on his arm.

He didn't seem to notice my silence, he was so busy telling me that he'd just heard the song was at number one. On and on he went, delirious with delight, crowing over who they'd knocked from the top spot, how many records they'd sold and what this meant for them now, according to Buzz Longhi. If there'd been a cardboard cut-out sitting next to him instead of me he wouldn't have noticed.

"It's all coming true at last," he went on, as the car slowed down then came to a standstill in front of the hotel where the party was to be held. "See those girls out there on the street, Chloe? They're waiting for me!"

A decent-sized crowd of yelling, screaming fans

— most of them round Lindsay's age, I would have said, plus a couple of seedy-looking photographers — were being kept firmly in check by a rope barrier and a couple of burly bouncers.

"Come on, let's make a dash for it," he yelled, grabbing my hand as he flung open the car door. We ran the gauntlet past the now hysterical fans to cries of "Greg! Greg!" and flashing cameras. Greg put one arm around me protectively and the other up to his face. He'd also slipped on a pair of shades, I noticed, although the night was pitch black. We sprinted the last few metres before the doors slid open to embrace us.

"How rock 'n' roll was that!" he yelled, holding on to my hand tight as we followed another bouncer whose job it was to lead us past the hoi polloi. These other party-goers — clearly excluded from the VIP area — followed our progress with expressions ranging from those of pretended indifference through to mild recognition and blatant envy. I couldn't believe how easily Greg seemed to be taking all this in his stride. It was like he'd been practising for this moment for a long time, and now that it had finally arrived, he was ready for it.

Just before we entered the VIP area Greg

grabbed hold of me, swung me round and planted a full-on kiss on my unsuspecting mouth. More cameras flashed, there was a storm of applause and a great deal of wolf-whistling and shrieking. The whole experience was getting more and more bizarre by the moment.

"That should give us the front pages in the tabloids tomorrow," he whispered.

A waiter sailed by and with the reflexes of a cat I reached out and grabbed two glasses of champagne. If I was going to confront Greg with Kendall's version of events, I needed Dutch courage and plenty of it.

"Chloe, you know I don't drink," Greg said and went to put one of the glasses back.

"Not bloody likely. These are for me. You can get your own," I retorted. Quick as a flash I knocked back the contents of one glass and immediately started on the other.

"Have I missed something here? I wasn't aware we were having a row," Greg said, his tone cautious.

I finished the other glass of champagne with even more speed than I'd drunk the first. OK, I could hold my own, but shampoo was a new one on me. I felt completely plastered already.

"For God's sake, why don't you take those shades off?" I hissed. "Who do you think you are? Bono?"

Greg snatched them off and slid them into his inside pocket. He might not have been the most sensitive of souls so far, but I think he'd managed to pick up that right now he was having the piss taken out of him, and he didn't like it. From the middle of the dance floor there came a roar of people enjoying themselves. I followed Greg's eyeline and spotted an extremely energetic Tillie right in the middle of the crowd, throwing herself around with the shrieking enthusiasm of an entire women's hockey team. From the wild ebullient cavorting she was trying to pass off as dancing, she was clearly well out of it. Gone was the languid, almost completely silent Tillie I'd first been introduced to back in December – coincidentally the day that I'd first met Greg.

"Mashed," he said. "No change there then." He turned back to me and rested his arms on my shoulders. He'd seen the way I'd looked at Tillie. Maybe he was beginning to piece two and two together. "Now, Chloe," he said. "Tell me. Please. What have I done?"

Tillie was lost to view now, but I could have sworn I could still hear her squealing from somewhere in the crowd. I pushed his hands away roughly and Greg staggered backwards with the force of it. "I've been talking to Kendall," I hissed. "I know all about Tillie, so don't even try to deny it."

His face seemed to shut down as my words registered with him. I prayed he'd swear to me that he had no idea what I was talking about, and that it would be the truth. But, when, after several moments of this blank stare, in which he appeared to be sifting through all the bits of information he suspected Kendall might be party to, and those which she couldn't possibly be, I just knew that Kendall had been speaking the truth.

"You clearly need a few more minutes to get your story right," I said. "I'm off to find the ladies' loo."

I headed off across the room, not really knowing where I was going, but finally I managed to locate the ladies'. I spent ages repairing my make-up and squirting myself with an assortment of fragrances that seemed to be there simply for the taking, just to avoid going back to Greg. A timid-looking foreign girl in a white coat turned on taps for people and handed them towels when they'd washed their hands.

I wondered how much she earned for performing such a menial task and how she must feel about having to do it. It was like she was invisible to everyone in the room. No one met her eyes, and no one thanked her for her trouble, being too intent on their own glossy reflections. *Is this what success and fame gives people?* I wondered. This ability to screen out anybody who was only there to wait on them? Clearly, warm smiles and hugs were only reserved for those who could further your career.

On my way out I beamed at the girl and said: "Thank you. You've been very kind."

She scowled back, clearly having me down as a rich, patronizing bitch. I felt embarrassed that I'd even considered a kind word from me might somehow fill her with gratitude.

chapter twenty-six

On my way back to find Greg, I was intercepted by someone calling my name, and spun round. It was Rob. He was dressed in a DJ like most of the men present, but his look came complete with kilt and sporran. He should have looked ridiculous, but with his height and breadth and his dark curls, he succeeded in carrying it off to swashbuckling effect. It was hard not to notice the number of female heads he was turning, although Rob clearly had no idea of the effect he was causing.

"Chloe!" He strained his voice above the racket.

I did my best to sound bright and breezy. "Rob! Good to see you," I said. "Did you come with Ewan McGregor? I thought I saw him on the way in."

Actually, this was a complete fabrication. Sofia had been right to say she wasn't expecting any big names.

Rob looked puzzled until I pointed out his kilt.

"Actually, it was the other way round," he joked. "Ewan McGregor came with me. Dreadful little hanger-on, that one. I keep telling him to piss off, but he keeps coming back."

"Like a boomerang, you mean?"

Rob pulled a face. "Fine," he said. "Get the Australian jokes out of the way first, then we don't have to refer to my nationality ever again."

"I'm sorry," I said. "It must be really annoying. Promise I'll never mention boomerangs or Rolf Harris or kangaroos ever again."

Rob grinned again. "You're forgiven, possum," he said. "Now, fancy a drink? Barman does the best cocktails this side of the Atlantic."

I thought of Greg waiting for me. "I shouldn't really," I began, but Rob's enthusiasm as he began to enumerate the number of cocktails he'd already sampled was catching. How uncomplicated it would be, to spend the rest of the evening propping up the bar with him and getting drunk! Easier than the prospect of going back to Greg.

"Oh, go on then, twist my arm," I said, hating myself for being such a coward. I should go back right now and have it out with him, I told myself. I knew I'd have to in the end, but for as long as it took to get served at the bar and drink one drink with Rob, I could kid myself that everything was just the same as it had been before Kendall decided to tell me otherwise.

We barged through the crowd to the bar. "Hey, mate! When you're ready!" he yelled at the barman.

The barman gave Rob a thumbs up and mouthed something that looked like "Thirty seconds" at him.

"Nice bloke, that," he said.

"Is he a pal of yours?"

"Not before tonight, but he's really interesting. He's doing a degree in Scandinavian Studies. There's nothing he can't tell you about the Vikings. Anyway, what about you? On your own?"

"Well, actually I'm with Greg. You know. Geffen. Tough Love."

I thought Rob seemed disappointed. But then two tall glasses of white liquid, chinking with ice, topped with foam and equipped with flame-orange straws were ceremoniously placed in front of us, saving the situation.

"Two Valhallas. Enjoy!" the barman said.

"Cheers, mate. Cheers, Chloe."

We raised our glasses and drank. I didn't know whether I liked what I was drinking or not, but it was certainly effective as an anaesthetic.

"What did he say it was called?" I asked Rob.

He shrugged. "Search me, but as long as it gets me pissed and I don't have to pay for it, then that's fine by me."

"A man after my own heart," I said and drank some more.

"You're certainly looking the part, tonight, Chloe," Rob said. "Apart from the white moustache you've developed above your top lip, that is."

I finished my drink and wiped my hand across my mouth. The drink was strong all right. In fact, it was just what I'd needed to make me look at things from a different angle. Surely there were two sides to every story. Why was Tillie's word worth more than Greg's? I owed it to him to hear him out, at least.

"Rob," I said. "I'm sorry, I have to go. Greg will be wondering where I am."

If he thought my manners were dreadful, he didn't say so, but only smiled graciously.

"Thanks for the drink. I owe you," I said, as I elbowed my way past him through the throng of drinkers all desperate to get as much free booze down their necks as possible.

Weaving my way back through the crowd to join Greg I couldn't locate him at first, my sense of direction slightly skewed by the amount of alcohol I'd knocked back. I must have wandered around for quite a while, before finally spotting him.

He was deep in conversation with Tillie, or rather she seemed to be haranguing him about something. Occasionally she swayed towards him and prodded him in the shoulder with her index finger.

My instinct was to make myself invisible in any way I could, so I sought refuge behind a potted plant, peeping through the foliage to see how events would pan out. Fortunately, whatever was happening was over almost as quickly as it had begun. I saw Greg reach out and grab Tillie's wrists. She struggled, there was a scuffle and then Kendall was on the scene. She threw Greg a look of pure hatred and spoke some words I couldn't catch. Greg and Tillie released each other from their mutual grip. Then Tillie collapsed, sobbing, into Kendall's arms. Kendall was clearly trying to comfort her as she led her away from Greg, who was now pretending that absolutely nothing unusual had happened. What on earth had been going on? And what was I supposed to do now?

There was only one thing for it. I decided to follow my instincts. I marched over to Greg and took his arm.

"Come on," I said. "We're leaving."

It was only when I said those words that Greg's mask of studied nonchalance slipped. He slumped towards me and buried his face in my neck, whispering, "Get me out of here, Chloe, and I promise I'll explain everything."

chapter twenty-seven

So, there we were, lying on Greg's narrow bed, back at the spartan apartment he shared with the rest of the band members. At last Greg's side of the story was told.

"There was never any official engagement between us," Greg insisted, when I told him the story Kendall had told me. "It was just some silly tabloid story she didn't bother denying. I was a pop star in waiting. What would I want with a wife? Then when she came back to me with this pregnancy story. . ." He shook his head wearily. "Listen, I'd long since stopped having sex with Tillie when she spun that yarn. She was far more interested in getting off her head than getting laid.

If she did sleep with someone it was probably only so she could blag a couple of lines of coke off him, and you can bet she wouldn't remember anything about it afterwards."

It was now two in the morning and it seemed like we – or rather Greg – had been talking for hours. He was clearly exhausted but I was wide awake. Every now and then I'd get up, pad into the eerily silent, sterile kitchen – where it looked like no one had even so much as dirtied a dish, let alone ever cooked a meal – and bring back two cups of strong, black coffee.

Greg's version was beginning to make sense to me. It certainly explained some of Tillie's weird behaviour. One minute unable even to open her eyes and say hello, like that first time I'd met her, the next minute throwing herself at me in the way she had at the launch party, like she'd known me all her life. And tonight, one minute the life and soul of the party, the next having to be dragged off Greg like that. With a drug habit like hers, it made sense she wouldn't remember who she shared a bed with.

Back in the bedroom again, I asked Greg, "Tell me again, when exactly did you meet Tillie?"

"Must have been at some party. Last year, some-time. We — the band — had just been signed and we were over the moon. Tilly was there. She always seemed to be at the same parties, for some reason. Anyway, on this particular night she was as high as a kite, though I guess I just didn't notice because so was I — although my mood had nothing to do with drugs. She just sort of — threw herself at me. I thought Christmas and my birthday had both come round at the same time."

"But it didn't stay like that?"

"I might be a rock 'n' roll star but drugs and booze have never featured in my life, Chloe. The music's always been enough for me to get off on. Not everybody can understand that."

"I know."

"All my life the only thing I ever wanted was to sing and to be famous for doing it. All the time my mates were out getting pissed or chatting up girls I was down the gym getting into shape, or practising in front of the mirror. I didn't have time for any of that other stuff, and getting signed like that changed nothing. It's just made me more deter-mined to get to the top and stay there."

"I'd no idea you had so much ambition. It must

be great to know exactly what you want from life so early on and just go for it."

I meant it. In fact I was plain jealous.

"Tillie and me were never big," Greg went on. "At first we had a laugh, that was all. But it wasn't long before I found out she couldn't enjoy herself without swallowing pills or booze or shoving something up her nose. Without that stuff she was just plain boring. Boring and neurotic and just like anybody else. She'd sold me a package she couldn't live up to. And when I told her I was getting fed up with her she went mental. Ugly. Really ugly. I felt, I don't know. . ." He hesitated before he spoke his next words, "Threatened by her. Like my life was in danger if I didn't give into her demands and stay with her. Sometimes I was so scared, Chloe."

"My God," I said. "Did she threaten to kill you?"

"Only when she was off her head," he said. Then he shuddered. "Even now I can't bear to think of those times. Give me a hug, Chloe. Make me forget those horrible times."

I held on to him as tightly as I could. Why had I doubted him over a drug addict? I must have been mad!

"And you really had broken off with Tillie the

day you gave me your phone number?"

"Hey! So that's what's worrying you. Ages before then." Greg kissed me gently on the nose. "I don't know how I'd have got through this business tonight if you hadn't been here to listen," he said. "You're a great girl, Chloe, honest."

"Don't be silly," I said.

"No, I mean it. You're not like those other girls. The Tillies. The Kendalls. The Sofias."

His hands had moved away from my hair to other parts of my body and although I felt I should have been resisting a bit more, I was enjoying his touch too much to put up a fight. With anyone else it would have been round about now that I would have called a halt, but with Greg, it just felt right.

"You are so lovely, Chloe. Do you know that? You're kind, you listen, you're funny, intelligent." He looked at me through narrowed eyes, a half smile on his face. My nerves were beginning to get the better of me. Briefly, I tried to fight it with a wisecrack.

"What about beautiful? You forgot beautiful."

"Mm. Beautiful goes without saying. Especially here. And here."

I edged away, not physically but mentally. Immediately Greg picked it up.

"Relax, Chloe. What's wrong? I swear, everything I've told you tonight is the truth. OK, maybe I should have told you sooner, but I couldn't risk putting you off with something so sordid as this. You're just too important to me."

"I believe you, Greg. Honest, it's not that I don't. It's just, well, there's something you should know about me."

"Mmm?"

"I'm still a virgin."

Briefly, very briefly, Greg paused.

"And do you want to remain one?"

My whole body yearned for him. If he stopped now, I thought I would die.

"No," I whispered. "No, I don't."

Greg kissed me again. "You're so sweet, babes," he said.

Afterwards, I felt soft and smug and satisfied. So this was what people made so much fuss about, I remember thinking, as moments later we drifted into sleep, folded close against each other, like two spoons in a drawer.

chapter twenty-eight

The following morning Greg and I came to consciousness almost at the same moment. For a minute or two I was consumed with awkwardness. How did you act when you found yourself naked in the same bed as the guy who had just taken your virginity? When I thought of everything that had happened between us the night before I wondered if I'd ever dare look Greg in the eye again. With my eyes tight shut, and keeping myself as far removed from him as the narrow bed allowed, I wondered just how I'd handle getting out of bed. I imagined the two of us creeping round each other's limbs while vainly attempting to cover up bits of ourselves with the duvet.

But it was all right. Greg had no qualms at all, which had the effect of putting me at my ease the moment he rolled over and tucked me into his arms to wish me good morning.

Half an hour later, I groped my way from beneath the duvet and grabbed Greg's shirt to wear as a nightie. I had no intention of being caught in the buff by any flatmates who might be wandering around. What I really wanted was a bath and I was desperate to clean my teeth. In the movies the beautiful people are still beautiful after a night of passion. Greg and I, on the other hand, were both distinctly scuzzy, and neither of us smelled too sweet. If we were going to kiss each other ever again then I had better find a toothbrush fast, I decided.

"I'm going to have to get over to Sofia's to drop this dress off and pick my stuff up," I mumbled, doing my utmost to gloss over the fact that wearing the same stuff I'd been wearing the night before was making me feel incredibly cheap. "My train ticket's there too, in my other bag."

Greg groaned at the mention of the house Sofia shared with Tillie and Kendall.

"I wouldn't expect you to come with me," I said.

Although actually I was desperate for his support. What were my chances against Tillie if she came running at me with the kitchen knife? I wondered. She was clearly missing a couple of slates, and if she had no qualms about threatening Greg, then I was pretty sure she'd have none about attacking me.

"I'll drive you," he said. "Though I won't come in. I don't trust myself."

While I made the coffee I wondered about what I'd say to Tillie, now I knew the whole story. Should I act as if nothing had happened last night, and as if – for all I knew – nothing had ever happened between her and Greg? And what if Kendall was there, which she probably would be? Odd, but it wasn't Tillie – for all I'd heard about her from Greg and in spite of what I'd witnessed with my own eyes – so much as Kendall that I felt threatened by. There was a calculating look about her that was extremely unnerving and made her much more menacing than the nebulous Tillie.

Of the three of them, Sofia was the only one who seemed capable of behaving like a normal human being, without some hidden agenda of her own. I'd have liked to stay and have a coffee with Sofia, maybe make arrangements to see her again.

But somehow, with either Tillie or Kendall likely to appear at any minute, I didn't think my visit would be more than a perfunctory one.

As it turned out, there was really no need for me to have got myself in such a state. Sofia was the only person up when I rang the bell – although clearly not the only person there. If Greg's house had been strangely empty of flatmates the night before, then it was pretty clear where at least two of them had slept.

The place was a tip, with overflowing ashtrays, dirty coffee cups, glasses and spilled wine on the coffee table. Someone had left a pair of men's shoes in the middle of the floor and CD's were scattered around the rug for anyone to trample on and break.

Sofia gave me a half-hearted bleary smile when she let me in. "The morning after the night before," she giggled, throwing me a look of complicity as she picked up the shoes and tidied them away under the coffee table.

"So who's here?" I asked, feigning sophistication, or so I hoped. I'd located my bag and was in the middle of checking that everything was as I'd left it.

"Don't ask me," she said. "Tillie insisted on dragging back a couple of boys from Tough Love. A reunion, she called it, after the video shoot. I ended up with Jake — or is it Jack? God knows. He's been hogging the bathroom for at least half an hour so I don't think there's much possibility of a cosy future together with him. Tillie's in there still with the other one." She cocked a look in the direction of Tillie's room, from where muffled sounds emerged, and raised her eyes heavenward.

"And Kendall?"

"Oh, it's Sunday," she said. "Never misses a home visit on Sundays, does Kendall."

Now that did surprise me.

"So you'll stay and have a coffee, then?"

I shook my head. "I have a train to catch, but thanks anyway. And tell Kendall thanks for the dress."

"Did it do the trick, then?"

I could feel myself blushing. "You could say that, I suppose," I admitted. My phone bleeped.

"Message from Greg. He wants me downstairs."

"His Master's Voice," Sofia said.

"Oh, he doesn't mean it like that," I said, wondering why I felt I had to defend him. "I think he's a bit worried in case Tillie decided to have a go at me."

"Tillie? Why would she want to do that?"

"Oh, you know. I'm with Greg now. She might not like it."

Sofia shrugged and looked a bit vague, as if it was the first she'd heard of Tillie ever having had anything to do with Greg. Well, perhaps it was. The three of them might share a flat together but it didn't mean they had to live in each other's pockets all the time, did it?

"You didn't see Tillie having a go at Greg last night, then?"

She answered quickly – rather too quickly I thought.

"Oh, I was too busy having a good time," she said, waving her arms around awkwardly. "Whatever upset Tillie she'd certainly forgotten about it by the time she got back here, so I wouldn't worry about it. Anyway, she always has a go at some poor sod when she's had a couple of drinks, although she would never say boo to a goose normally. She was probably just tired and emotional."

"Yeah, you're probably right," I said. Clearly,

Sofia wouldn't be drawn to say anything negative about Tillie. It would be nice to have Sofia for a friend, I decided, if she was always so loyal.

Then, as if to disabuse of me of this fancy notion, she immediately added: "As a newt!"

We both dissolved into giggles which immediately dispersed the awkwardness. After saying our goodbyes and making promises to meet up sooner rather than later, I ran downstairs into Greg's embrace.

"To the station, James," I quipped.

"You can't go home," he said, as he put the car into gear. "I won't let you. I want you on my arm at the party tonight. What sort of a sad bastard will I look if I go to my own party alone?"

"We've been through this already, Greg," I sighed, as indeed we had. "I can't miss college tomorrow or my dad will go ballistic."

"I'll talk to your dad," he offered. "He seems like a reasonable man."

I almost slid out of my seat. "Are we talking about the same man here?" I demanded. "My dad would make Ghengis Khan seem like Sergeant Wilson."

Greg looked perplexed. He was clearly not a devotee of "Dad's Army".

"Come back to the flat and have a cup of tea, Chloe. Then at least we can say goodbye properly."

I agreed, thinking no harm could possibly come of that — I'd just catch a later train, that was all. But I hadn't bargained on Greg's persistence, not to mention the persuasive ways with which he shamelessly enticed me back into his bedroom, even before the tea in my cup was cool enough to drink.

There was nothing for it. I would have to ring home and tell a lie.

Whoever picks up the phone, don't let it be Dad, I prayed, as I listened to the dialling tone. Greg was meant to be out of the room, making some tea which this time he'd promised he'd let me drink, but he kept popping his head back round the door to check that I was doing what I'd said I'd do.

"Mum?"

"That you, Chloe?" There was an edge to her voice. "Thank God for that."

The best strategy would be to get it over with, I decided. I took a deep breath and went for it. "Listen. The girls have asked me to stay on an extra night. Some party or other."

Mum didn't respond for ages. Finally she said: "Where will you be staying?"

My God, she knew. I was sure she knew exactly where I was making the call from, what I'd been doing and most certainly who with. Greg appeared at the door, wearing nothing but a towel and carrying a tray of tea things. I shushed him and waved him away but he kept on coming.

"With Sofia. Like I said," I lied.

"Lucky for you I picked the phone up and not your dad, that's all I can say, my girl," Mum grumbled. "Just you be careful, that's all."

I was momentarily stunned. Where were the hysterics, where was the summons home, why the ready consent, as if all I'd asked for was permission to go on a college trip?

"So it's OK, is it?"

"I suppose so. Although what about college?"

A weary note had crept into her voice, almost as if she felt obliged to bring up the subject of my education, but couldn't quite summon up the enthusiasm to beat me up over the prospect of missing double English.

"Mum, are you all right?"

A beat, then: "I'm fine. It's Lindsay I'm worried about."

"Oh? What's happened?"

"She passed out. One minute she was talking to me about something she'd read in a magazine about grains or something. Next she's on the floor."

"When did this happen?" Mentally I tried to work out when I'd last seen Lindsay eating anything. I hadn't seen her at all on Saturday, although she'd been around the table on Friday eating her meal with the rest of us, surely? I suppose I'd been so busy scoffing and thinking about the weekend that I'd taken little notice of her.

"This morning. I've sent her back to bed. I thought about taking her to see the doctor in the morning, but she's adamant there's nothing wrong with her. Do you think she's eating properly?"

I had to admit that it didn't look like it.

"I can't think what's come over her lately," Mum went on. "She always used to be so good with her food. Even when she was a baby. It was you who was always the fussy one."

"Well, it can't do any harm to take her to the surgery," I said. "Maybe they can suggest a more sensible way for her to lose weight."

"But she doesn't need to lose weight, Chloe. She's fine as she is."

Greg coughed. "HURRY UP," he mouthed.

"Listen, Mum, someone's just made me a cup of tea. I'd better drink it before it gets cold. But take her anyway."

"Yes, I intend to. See you tomorrow then. And don't you come back with something else for me to worry about, will you?"

"MUM! I've no idea what you're talking about."

She sniffed, wished me goodbye again, and hung up.

"So you're coming to the party with me, then?"

"Looks like it."

"What's up?"

I pulled Greg down on to the bed. "Nothing," I insisted. "Honestly."

Right then, when I had an opportunity to confide in Greg, I found I didn't know where to start. I wanted to forget everything. College, exams, parents, Tillie, Kendall, Lindsay — everything but the moment and Greg.

chapter twenty-nine

After we slept together, my feelings for Greg changed completely. The act of making love with him had plunged me headlong into a swirling surf of crazy emotions. I'd been transformed by his sure touch and now his power over me was total. I was dizzy with desire for him. I'd become like some super-charged creature — a greyhound, a thorough-bred racehorse — a network of nerves, quiveringly alert to every external stimulus. I'd never thought about sex much before — I'd even thought there must be something wrong with me because I didn't — but now I thought about it all the time.

I saw his face before me all the time, and the sound of his voice was in my head constantly, as if part of my brain were grooved with his voice pattern, activated by the electric charge of memory. But it would be six weeks at least until I saw him next. How could I still my body again, after he'd so expertly awakened it?

And how on earth was I going to fill the time? Lucky for me that Olympus, in the form of Serena Montague, gave me an alternative to swotting French verbs and the date of the Treaty of Versailles. A couple of days before term ended she called with a whole day's worth of casting appointments.

"I know your term must end very soon and because you don't live in town I've tried my best to get these castings back to back for you so you won't have to come up two days on the trot. If you get any of these jobs you'll be working in the holiday anyway, so you won't get me into trouble with your parents."

I was delighted at the prospect of doing more modelling, not least because it would take my mind off Greg.

"You know I really admire the way you've put your studies first right from the beginning, Chloe. There are so many silly girls in this business who let modelling go straight to their heads. Any ideas they had of pursuing college just fall by the wayside at the first sight of a celebrity boyfriend. Then five years down the line when the jobs drop off and the celebrity boyfriend's moved on, they're kicking themselves for wasting their education."

I could feel myself blushing. If only Serena knew just how close, recently, I'd been to jacking in college! After the Easter vacation I had just three or four weeks left and then it would be study leave and I'd be free to take on as many jobs as I was offered until I started my exams – it was only this realization that had kept me going.

"You stick with it, Chloe. I'm sure you don't need me to tell you that there's no substitute for an education."

"Oh, absolutely," I said, although I'd rarely felt so unenthusiastic about anything for a long time.

My enthusiasm for the castings, however, was boundless. I struck lucky with all of them. The first was for a fashion shoot for a glossy magazine I'd seen on the shelves but had always thought was full of clothes that were way out of my league. Well, now it seemed that I'd be modelling them. The shoot was to take place the following week and I would be expected to give up a whole day for the job.

Maybe all this enthusiasm paid off, because I was booked for the next casting too. Party-wear for a High Street chain that would be in the shops for Christmas. My picture would be plastered on the walls of every outlet of the well-known High Street retail store and on top of that I'd be on billboards across the country too! I was ecstatic! By Christmas I would be a familiar face in every household!

Then came my final casting – for yet another glossy.

"The whole issue will be devoted to weddings," I was told. "Now, you won't be the bride, because we've already booked her, but you will be a guest, and very possibly a bridesmaid."

Clearly, I was going to be very busy. And very rich. I rang Greg to tell him that night.

"No way! I'm well impressed," he said, when I told him my face was going to be plastered over billboards and magazines all over the country. "Now there's no danger of me forgetting your face."

"Well, there's no way I could forget yours," I

said. "Every time I open a magazine or switch on the TV you seem to be there. I just wish you were here instead."

"Where is here exactly?"

"In my room," I sighed. "In my bed."

Greg gave a low chuckle. "Well, there's a coincidence. Because that's where I am, too."

It may sound as if I was totally obsessed with Greg and sex at this time, but I did leave a bit of room in my busy modelling life to keep up with Lindsay. True to her word, Mum had hauled her off to see Doctor Stafford, our ageing GP, who'd listened to Mum's explanation as to why Lindsay had fainted, then promptly turned to Lindsay and told her not to be so silly ever again. As far as he could see she was a perfectly proportioned young woman, who just needed to pull herself together and use the intelligence God gave her to feed herself when she was hungry, and put a stop to "this slimming nonsense".

I wouldn't have thought that this advice would be particularly helpful to someone who was convinced they looked like a carthorse and who'd gone along to the surgery – albeit reluctantly – with at least a faint hope that they could be helped in some way. To everyone's surprise, though, it actually seemed to do the trick. Within hours, Lindsay stopped talking about food and started coming to the table again. Mum relaxed and stopped watching her like a hawk every time she lifted her fork to her mouth, and mealtimes became a much calmer affair now that Lindsay was no longer the centre of attention.

And funnily enough, Lindsay, now she'd stopped obsessing about food to all and sundry, appeared to be losing a bit of weight into the bargain, so the problem seemed to have resolved itself.

chapter thirty

My third job in just under two weeks and I was becoming a pro. The feedback I'd received from the agency about my Christmas shoot and the first editorial were both really positive, so it was with a light heart that I found myself, with about two hundred others – men and women of all ages, a gaggle of children (including a couple of tiny babies) and models my age – being briefed for the shoot, which would entail us being bussed from one location to another in an attempt to convey a traditional, if extremely upper-crust, English wedding.

The day was perfect. The sun shone in a clear blue sky that meant shooting outside was going to be a breeze. The church was ideal according to the photographer – part Norman, part something else, but he couldn't remember what. The marquee was finally up – they'd been erecting it since dawn, apparently – and the wedding buffet was being laid out as we spoke. There was one problem, though. The bride hadn't turned up.

We all chuckled at this – as you would, of course, and jokes about the groom being stood up abounded for the first half-hour or so. But the merriment soon dissolved when it became clear that the bride's absence was not part of the script, but a very serious misdemeanour indeed on the part of the model who was supposed to be playing her.

Apparently there'd been a series of phone calls to the girl, but so far she hadn't picked any of the calls up and now they were on to her agent, or so the buzz went in the changing room where I was squashed alongside half a dozen other girls. (One thing I'd learned very quickly in my brief career as a fashion model was that *all* changing rooms, without exception, were too small, and were invariably either too hot or too draughty.) Today we all shivered through our flimsy gowns and peep-toed shoes, in much the same way probably that those bridesmaids and wedding guests would themselves be doing when they eventually donned these outfits at some real English summer wedding.

We'd been sitting around for quite a while now – something else which I'd learned to take in my stride – waiting for the hitch to be smoothed out. People exchanged opinions about what they thought would happen if they couldn't locate her. The photographer had already taken several shots – though none of me in my bridesmaid's outfit, which I was very sorry about because it meant I didn't dare pop to the loo or disappear to the makeshift canteen, in case I slopped mayonnaise all down the front of my £3000 dress – and although it would be possible to take pictures of the bride alone at a later date, he needed at least a dozen shots of her with the groom and assembled guests. Clearly the phenomenal expense caused by reassembling everyone would make that impossible.

"You know who it is, of course, don't you?" someone wearing an apple-green hat with a brim wide enough to knock the top tier off the wedding cake, asked me. "I've heard it's not the first time she's done this sort of thing, either."

I shrugged to indicate I hadn't a clue who the offender was. All I knew was that I wouldn't have been in her shoes for the world. Since I'd joined Olympus I'd had so many lectures about professional behaviour winning a girl more jobs than any amount of beauty or talent, that I'd become paranoid about setting off in the morning at least an hour before I needed to just in case I got stuck in traffic.

"Tillie Asher, she's called. Started out with big hopes last year. Between you and me and the tabloids she's been hitting the buffers for quite a while now. Too many parties and too much bed-hopping. You know, usual story."

I felt my blood run cold. I thought about Serena tearing her hair out when she learned that one of her models hadn't turned up for a shoot. I'd never seen her lose her rag, but I wouldn't want to be around when she did, that was for sure.

"Is there a Chloe Dove here?" A girl dressed in jeans and leather jacket who'd been ticking off names on a list when we'd arrived — which was now beginning to feel like three weeks ago — scurried in officiously.

"Whoops, Chloe, what have you been up to? She's over here," green-hat called out.

The girl in jeans bustled over. "The photographer and the magazine editor would like to see you, pronto," she said.

I gawped up at her, village-idiot-style.

"Now," she hissed, clearly asking herself why she'd fallen for the hype about jobs in the media offering the opportunity for a glamorous lifestyle.

Gathering my skirts about me, I hitched myself out of my chair and lurched after her, cursing, as more than once I caught one or other of my heels in the hem. The girl with jeans was practically out of sight, it was taking me so long to make progress.

"Sorry," I panted. "Not used to these heels. What do they want me for? Have I done something wrong?"

She grinned at me. "*Au contraire*," she said, mangling the words as only someone whose first language was English can do. "But I'll let them tell you. Here we are."

"Ah, Chloe." The magazine editor, I presumed — since I hadn't seen her before — extended a languid arm and waved it about vaguely in my direction. She turned to the photographer who was peering at me through one of his lenses. "She's a very different type to the other one, isn't she? A bit more sparky, I'd say. The other one always looked like a bit of a victim."

The photographer nodded. "It'll mean some readjustment to my vision," he said. Had I missed something here or was he employed to take a few snaps? To hear him talk this production was the next *Titanic*.

The editor widened her eyes, sympathetically. "Can it be done, though? What do you think? I mean, you're the one who's got to work with her, after all."

I wondered how much longer they were going to carry on like this and what on earth it was to do with me? Finally, after more hesitation, in which he seemed to be weighing up any number of pros and cons, the photographer made a small moue of acceptance.

"Selina's sent some brill references. Highly intelligent, learns quickly though she's not had that much experience, that sort of thing. What do you think, Chloe? How quickly can you get out of those clothes and into the bridal outfit?"

I blinked, opened my mouth and shut it again.

They wanted me to be the bride! The star of the shoot! My insides started to fizz with barely containable glee.

"It'd mean the cover too," the magazine editor added. "Your money would be doubled, but we've already talked to Serena about that. What do you say?"

I didn't need to give it another thought. "I say show me the dress," I grinned.

I was so caught up in the moment, wondering how soon I could get to my phone and ring Greg to tell him my news that I didn't take much notice of the kerfuffle behind me. Until I heard a familiar voice – loud, barely polite and with a jagged edge of East End London poking through sharp enough for someone to slit their throat on.

"I've brought her here to apologize. If you'll still let her, she'll get changed. Tillie. Get over here."

It was Kendall, all fired up and ready for battle, with a clearly contrite Tillie taking refuge several metres behind her.

chapter thirty-one

There was an audible silence during which time several things occurred. The magazine editor, the photographer and the girl in jeans exchanged coded looks which meant absolutely nothing to me but were clearly a signal for the three of them to take up their fighting corners. It was almost as if they'd half expected something like this to happen, and they were ready for it.

The girl in jeans hooked her arm under mine and propelled me right away from the scene so the opportunity to come face to face with Kendall never even presented itself, which was a huge relief as far as I was concerned. I did catch sight of Tillie, though – looking more waif-like than ever I remembered her, the dark shadows beneath her heavy-lidded eyes doing surprisingly little to detract from her frail beauty. She threw me a look of such piteous dismay that I almost felt like running over to her and telling her there and then that I was relinquishing the opportunity to take over from her, and I would have done, but for the vicious tweak of the elbow I received from the girl in jeans.

"Stay out of it," she hissed. "They wouldn't have her now if she prostrated herself, trust me."

The magazine editor threw up her hands in pained despair and said in a tight, clipped voice: "You could have saved yourself the petrol, my dear. It's very sweet of you to drag your little friend all this way but clearly she's in no fit state to appear in any photo, other than perhaps a Wanted poster."

She smirked at the photographer, clearly delighted by her own joke.

"She'll be fine, honest. She gets this allergy — wheat. Makes her sick. But with a bit of make-up. . ."

There was some hollow laughter from the photographer, followed by a smothered exchange behind their hands between him and the magazine editor.

"Chloe, come on. Let me get you back into the changing room," my jailer hissed in my ear. "We can't waste any more time."

I wish I'd been allowed to stay and to hear the rest of the pathetic excuses Kendall must have made for Tillie, not to mention what Tillie herself had to say for herself, but clearly at this late stage no amount of grovelling apology would change things. I was the new bride and Tillie was nada. I dreaded to think what Kendall would do when she found out it was me who'd taken the job from under her best friend's nose, and for the first time since I'd donned it I was grateful for the headdress I was wearing, which shielded me from view. Meekly, I followed the girl in jeans back to the changing room in order to collect my stuff and move into the dressing room that had been assigned to Tillie.

Stop it now, I told myself, as I struggled out of one gown and into another. I had nothing to apologize for, I reminded myself, I wasn't the one who'd got off my face the previous night. If I wasn't careful I'd find myself right back in pathetic mode, which was exactly where I'd started from with Kelly — guilty because I'd been singled out for glory, apologetic because poor Tillie had had the job snatched from under her nose and, above all else, unable to make the most of a situation most girls would give their eye teeth for. If I'd learned anything over the past few months it was that I was as good as anybody else. Hadn't someone said that one day I'd be on the cover of *Vogue*? Hadn't Serena herself recommended me for this job today, when half the models on the shoot were employees of Olympus?

It was with my pep talk to myself in mind that I posed for the photographer. In a pensive mood at the open French window, as my "father" adjusted my veil. Radiant, as I strolled out of the church with my new life partner. Full of fun, as I threw my bouquet over my shoulder, aiming it in the direction of my "best friend". Flirtatious, as I took to the floor with my husband and we danced in each other's arms for the camera. (Let me tell you about male models, while I'm on the subject. They are all, to a man, too boring for words. With that in mind, I won't be expending any more words on them.)

The entire shoot sped by like a perfect dream with nothing but praise from the photographer as I followed his every direction effortlessly. Up until now I'd never really felt completely at ease with myself as I posed for pictures – I was no actor, after all. But today everything fell into place. It was like I'd suddenly broken in a new pair of shoes and the stiffness had gone at last. I was in my trustiest slippers and I could have danced all night.

"Satisfied?" the photographer asked me, at the very end of the day, as we all tucked into the edible remains of the wedding buffet.

I grinned and nodded enthusiastically through a mouthful of – alas – now rather stale cake.

"So you should be," he said. "We couldn't have done this in one day if you hadn't been so utterly professional. You'll get a lot of work after this, you mark my words. I'll see to it myself."

I was flattered. I was happy. In fact I was positively delirious. All it would have taken for the day to turn out to be perfect would have been to talk to Greg, but he was filming somewhere that day. The only thing that lay ahead for me was a train journey home, a mug of cocoa and bed.

If only I lived in London, I remember thinking, as I packed away my bits and pieces and climbed back into the coach that was going to take us back to central London. But that seemed as remote a possibility to me right then as fitting in two hours of revision before I went to sleep. Bagging a window seat, I made a little pillow for myself with my rolled-up sweater and drifted into sleep, as the events of the day danced around my head.

chapter thirty-two

Back at college, my first exam, quiet nights and routine-led days, punctuated with periods of lying on my bed dreaming and counting the days until I could see Greg again. When I was free at weekends, he was booked for something, when he had a couple of days off midweek, whaddya know, I had two exams one after the other.

We talked on the phone, we sent texts back and forth, but there's basically something extremely dissatisfying about a relationship conducted in that way and I'm sure I'm not the only person ever to have come to that realization. If you don't share experiences, how can you relive them? If you don't know the same people, who's there to talk about?

If you live in different worlds — and right now Greg and I couldn't have been inhabiting realms which were further apart — then what shared vocabulary exists?

Sometimes I felt we didn't even speak the same language. Greg wasn't interested in my exams — he'd made it clear he had no interest in anything remotely connected with education, actually — and though he was pleased about my modelling success, I found myself unable even to open up to him about that, because if I'd done so I'd have been forced to explain Tillie's rôle in my good fortune. The less said about her the better!

I kept telling myself not to be so gloomy, and that the next time I clapped eyes on Greg again, any doubts I had about being able to sustain a relationship with someone who had such different preoccupations to my own would just vanish.

Meanwhile, in order to divert my thoughts away from him, I took to studying Lindsay. I guess my suspicions had been roused by the way she'd so meekly appeared to acquiesce to the doctor's prescription of NO MORE DIETING. Lindsay never went along with anything if she thought it was something her elders and betters wanted, so why had the house so far failed to resound with her screams of "Not fair" and "What gives anyone the right to tell me what to eat?" Something wasn't right, I was certain.

Let me remind you of my theory that everyone believes themselves to be the centre of the universe. The one that says there's no point worrying about your appearance or your behaviour, because no one other than you will ever notice your faults or even remember very much about you at all, in fact.

Well, this theory is all-embracing. It also applies to food. In our house, in common I suspect with millions of other homes, no one ever noticed how much or how little anybody else ate because they were all too busy shovelling it away themselves, or, in Lindsay's case, too busy thinking up tactics to avoid eating anything at all. After the initial fuss over what Lindsay ate, when Mum stood over her and practically spooned the stuff into her mouth, eating patterns returned pretty much to normal in our house.

No one ever ate a proper breakfast, we all just grabbed what we had time for. Lunch was eaten outside the house for the most part, or was combined with breakfast to make a casual brunch at the weekend – again, on an individual basis.

A casual observer would have sworn, if asked, that whatever was on Lindsay's plate was definitely dwindling bit by bit, but the evening meal presented me with the perfect opportunity to observe exactly how skilled Lindsay was becoming at not eating anything at all.

Normally, I ate anything and everything put in front of me, and quickly, as I was always in competition with Dad for seconds of roast potatoes and meat. If I'd shadowed anyone's eating habits before, then it had been his. But I must have picked up some kind of bug from the wedding shoot – something to do with nibbling at snackettes that had been left too long under hot lights, I guessed, although I was in no position to sue as I had been warned of the likely consequences. Now, I was seriously off my food. Although I still sat round the table – anyone's company was better than my own when I'd been working all day – I ate little, and soon found myself observing exactly how Lindsay dealt with dinner.

I learned plenty, and I had to admit that she was very good. She had Mum and Dad fooled, that was for sure. First of all she helped herself to minuscule amounts of absolutely everything on offer, even the stuff she hated that not even Mum would have forced her to eat, so that by the time she'd finished replacing lids and handing dishes back and forth, the steam had disappeared from most of the stuff on her plate.

Then she cut everything up into pieces as tiny as she could manage and proceeded to mash them to a slurry with the back of her fork. By degrees, the amount disintegrated and soon began to appear much less than it had when it was in solid lumps, although – and this was a stroke of genius – she left whole the food she had Mum's permission NOT to eat, the sprouts, the pastry corners, the fat around the meat and so on.

Meanwhile, she kept up a barrage of conversation, all dreary stuff about what Tracey Butterworth had said to Miss Newcombe and how fit the new science teacher was, which seemed to amuse Mum and Dad no end. During her monologue, Mum and Dad would manage to clear their plates and Dad might even be digging around for seconds.

After Lindsay had pushed the mixture round her

plate for a while longer, Mum would start on her "Well, I've done my bit so now it's your turn to clear up" routine. Whereupon Lindsay would leap out of her seat as keenly as if she'd been offered tickets for a weekend at EuroDisney (I know, but there's no accounting for taste) and volunteer to do everything herself, since Dad was clearly exhausted and I'd got my swotting to do. Often, she'd add that it would give her a chance to scrape the pan out, or help herself to what was left of the bread and butter, or pick at the chicken or whatever else she could come up with to convince Mum and Dad that her appetite was nothing if not gargantuan.

You had to ask yourself, were Mum and Dad stupid or what? I couldn't understand why Mum's antennae weren't sparking with suspicion. I mean, Lindsay had stopped volunteering years ago, when she'd finally cottoned on that what the word actually meant was that you did something without getting any money for doing it. She'd have been about seven then.

chapter thirty-three

One afternoon, I decided to have it out with her. Mum and Dad weren't in yet and I'd been in the garden all afternoon, ostensibly swotting but in reality dozing on my sunbed. The day had become hot, just like it invariably did when exams were on, and earlier I'd got changed into my bikini top and shorts. If I was a model then surely I ought to think about getting a tan, I reasoned. The change in weather was having no effect on Lindsay, though. She was still wrapped up in jeans and layers of droopy vest tops and T-shirts, topped off with a shapeless shirt, which I had started to assume was part of a grunge look she clearly – if mistakenly – thought looked attractive.

"Warm enough for you?" I asked her. I handed her the bowl of ice cream I'd prepared for her.

She looked up from her magazine and frowned when she saw what I was holding out.

"That's not for me, is it?" she said.

"Come on, Linds. It's your favourite. Chocolate chip. Two scoops."

I could see the little cogs in her brain working overtime, wondering how on earth she could get out of this one. She must have realized there was no way I'd believe her if she told me she'd already had ice cream today because this was the first of a new tub.

I'd already tolerated the fib she'd told just before lunch about having had a HUGE breakfast while I'd been in bed so she wasn't ready for a sandwich yet. I'd even had the cunning to say to her that if she wasn't hungry now, then maybe we could have a bowl of ice cream later. She'd muttered an OK, probably assuming I wouldn't pursue it, but now I'd called her bluff.

I sat down on the blanket next to her and waited until she came to the realization that she had no alternative but to accept my offering.

"Come on then, dig in. Yummy, isn't it?"

Yummy was not a word I'd allowed into my vocabulary store for at least ten years, but I was desperate. I started in on my first scoop. It was pretty good ice cream, actually, and I began to convince myself there were worse words.

"Mmm," she said, "although I think I prefer the strawberry to this one. And have you tried the pistachio?"

Lindsay's avoidance tactics were coming into play now. I only half listened as she described the flavour of every individual ice cream this particular range offered and went on to compare it to similar flavours produced by different brands. I was more interested in watching the way she liquidized the mixture with her spoon, twirling it round and round the bowl as she spoke. By the time I'd finished mine, I doubt whether one single spoonful had passed Lindsay's lips.

"I know what you're doing, you know," I said. "You may be able to fool Mum and Dad, but you can't fool me."

She froze, clearly unprepared for a confrontation. "I don't know what you're talking about," she said. "God, look what I've done with this. It's all melted now." She put the spoon to her mouth, tasted a minuscule amount then grimaced. "I can't eat it now I've made such a mess of it," she added.

"Lindsay. Will you just stop it. I know you're still not eating, even though you've been told by the doctor that you don't need to lose weight."

I happened to catch sight of her arms. She'd been wearing long sleeves all winter, naturally, but the unaccustomed heat of today must have forced her to roll up her sleeves. I made a grab for her wrist and spanned it between thumb and forefinger. Lindsay yelped and tried to free herself but I clung on.

"Has Mum seen this?"

Finally, Lindsay managed to snatch her arm free. "I need to lose weight, Chloe. What does that stupid doctor know? Anyway, it's all right for you, you've always been skinny."

"Lindsay, for Chrissake, you're thinner than I am by miles. Just look at your arms!"

She muttered something about her thighs and bum being as big as an elephant's and still having half a stone to lose.

"Then I'll stop." I challenged her with a look. "I will. I promise," she insisted.

I could have walked away and left her to it. I'd

done so in the past and I could do it now. I wasn't her mother, after all, and if Mum didn't think there was a problem then shouldn't I just let things rest? No, I couldn't. I'd read about anorexics and I'd seen films about them.

Until now I'd thought that Lindsay was just a silly kid trying to lose a bit of weight, which admittedly she'd needed to do at one time. But this was different. She was thin enough, now. Too thin. Anorexics never thought you could be thin enough, I knew that much. If Lindsay lost seven more pounds – a whole half stone – would she suddenly decide she could do with losing a bit more? Where would it end?

I took a sneaking, sidelong look at her and tried to picture what she looked like beneath all those layers of clothing she still insisted on wearing even on such a hot day. Why didn't she take them off and lap up the sun, as I was doing? Something clicked inside my brain. It wasn't because she thought she was too fat, but rather the opposite. If she removed all those layers of clothing all of us would finally realize just how much weight she'd lost over the last few months.

"Lindsay, it's got to stop, you know. I'm going to

have to talk to Mum as soon as she comes home."

"What does she care?" Lindsay snapped. Her face was turning red — either because she was too hot in all those clothes, or she was getting sunburned, or maybe a combination of both.

Her words shocked me. "She's your mother, Lindsay. Of course she cares. She trusted you to do as the doctor advised, as you would expect to be trusted, surely, and you've thrown that trust back in her face."

"Well, if she's such a good mother then how come you're the one that's giving me the pep talk?" Lindsay threw me a look of triumph.

I didn't know the answer to that. Who did? Maybe Mum thought the subject was closed, it had been dealt with. Maybe she preferred to believe those things, so she wouldn't have the chore of standing over Lindsay while she ate, alongside the other hundred and one tasks she had to do in the space of a day. I felt a twinge of guilt at my own part in this. Basically, we were all as lazy as each other in my family, and never thought of doing anything until we were asked. *Must do better*, I told myself sternly, then started on Lindsay again. It was time to lay it down hot and strong.

"Do you have any idea what happens to anorexics?"

She wrinkled her brow. "I'm not anorexic," she muttered.

So on top of everything else, she was in denial. Well, no one could help her until she faced up to the fact, I was certain of that.

"If you carry on like this then your whole system will pack up. You haven't finished growing yet. You need calcium for your bones and teeth and you need proper nourishing food for your brain and your nervous system."

"Spare me the biology lesson."

"Sooner or later your periods will stop and in the future – should you live that long – you won't be able to have children. Towards the end you'll start to grow hair all over your body. But the hair on your head will probably fall out. Your kidneys will fail, then your heart, and then you'll die."

At last I seem to have struck a chord. Lindsay looked horrified now, just like she used to when she was little and I'd tell her ghost stories when we were in bed. Then she spoke, in a tiny, strangled voice. "I don't want to do this. But I can't help it. I don't want to die."

I hugged Lindsay to me, and felt how thin she'd become through the material of her clothes. We had to do something now, before things got any worse.

"I'll talk to Mum," I said. "She'll get you some proper help."

Lindsay shook her head frantically. "No, Chloe. Don't tell Mum, please. She'll go mad."

"She won't go mad, don't be stupid. Or if she does go mad it'll be with herself for not noticing anything."

"She doesn't care about me. If I did die she'd probably be relieved. I'm just a boring dumpy schoolgirl with no talent. Not beautiful and clever like you. With your modelling career and a boyfriend who's in a rock band."

So we were finally getting to the bottom of this. "Lindsay, you're talking absolute rot," I told her. "Mum and Dad love you to bits. Just think of the way you make them laugh all the time. I've seen both of them weeping at one of your stories. I can't do that. You've got a real way with words, I've always thought that. Mum says she wouldn't be surprised if you turn out to be a writer or something."

Lindsay widened her eyes in disbelief. Either because it was the first time she could remember that I'd ever said anything nice to her, or because she sincerely had no idea how much she was appreciated by Mum and Dad for her funny little ways — I don't know which.

"Just because we don't go round like the Waltons telling each other we love each other all the time it doesn't mean we don't," I said.

Lindsay seemed to be turning things over in her head. She was silent for some time, and had extricated herself from my hug. Now she withdrew some distance away and said:

"Chloe. Will you help me first? Give me a chance. Please, don't tell Mum."

She looked at me with such desperate pleading in her eyes that I almost relented. I could watch her and make food for her and sit with her while she ate it. But what if she was just bluffing and started to slide back just like she'd done before? The responsibility was just too much for one person. This was a burden I couldn't take on all by myself.

chapter thirty-four

Mum wasn't as surprised to hear what I had to say as I'd thought she would be. She sat at the kitchen table pushing a half-empty glass of water round in circles and staring straight ahead of her. Lindsay was still out in the garden, probably too afraid to come inside.

"I got a call yesterday from Lindsay's year tutor to go in and see her. That's where I've been now. The school. They're worried that Lindsay might have some kind of eating disorder. She'd fainted a couple of times after PE and they got suspicious as she seems a bit lethargic in class too. And of course, she's lost so much weight, which I hadn't noticed because I've probably not been looking after her as closely as I should have been." There was a bitter edge to Mum's weary voice.

"It's been frantic at work, recently," she continued. "Ofsted, reports. It's easy to forget you've got kids if they're not sniffing glue or robbing old ladies. I guess I've always thought you two could just be left to your own devices and you'd be all right."

"Mum, this is not your fault," I said. "This is Lindsay with some mad idea that you love me more than you love her. She thinks she's a failure, all the more so since I've been modelling."

"A failure!" Mum threw up her hands in horror. "She's thirteen, for goodness' sake! And what have I ever done to make her think I favour one of you over the other? What must she think of me?"

"Mum, don't blame yourself," I pleaded. "It's not your fault. I know it must be hard for you but you've got to be strong for Lindsay's sake."

"I know that, Chloe. Which is why I've already contacted the hospital. They've given me the name of someone who might help. Unfortunately," she added, bitterly, "because Lindsay's not quite dead yet they can't admit her to the centre that deals with young people with eating disorders."

"But she can get professional help?"

Mum nodded. "Counselling, that kind of thing. Your dad and I will go to any lengths to get her cured of this. But she has to own up to it first, the counsellor says. A bit like an alcoholic, you know. Unless you can stand up and admit that's what you are, then you'll never stand a chance of being cured."

"Well, I think I can promise you that she hates the way she is round food. She really does want to change."

Mum sniffed and swallowed hard. She was clearly at that stage that if you allow one sob or one tear to escape, then you won't be able to stop yourself flooding the entire room. I thought it better not to say any more about it.

"I'll make a cup of tea," I said.

She gave me a weak smile. "Thanks, Chloe," she said. "You're a good girl for taking Lindsay on like this. You've handled it really well. At one time you'd have gone at it like a bull in a china shop."

"Well, I'm an adult now," I said, and smiled back.

"I suppose you are."

There was a companionable silence between us

as I bustled about my business, filling the kettle, setting a tray with mugs and filling a plate with digestive biscuits while Mum sat and stared out of the window or continued to turn the glass round and round in her hands. I actually felt grown up, and even – briefly – that I'd taken some of Mum's responsibility for Lindsay's recovery on to myself. After all, somewhere at the bottom of this lay Lindsay's firm, if irrational belief that I was the favoured child.

I tried to see myself through her eyes. I'd have been guilty of gross false modesty if I'd failed to see just why she could envy me. My life was looking good right now. I'd had word from Serena that the wedding shoot had been a huge success and that the editor of that magazine was keen to sign me up for a whole series of fashion shoots.

Perhaps I'd gloated a bit too much about my success and maybe this had contributed to Lindsay's feelings of inadequacy by comparison. I blushed to the roots of my hair when I remembered some of the things I'd called her in the past. How could I have been so insensitive? It was time to make amends.

When she appeared at the back door, hesitant

253

about coming in, Mum and I both looked up and smiled at her. Lindsay looked from one to the other of us, and spoke accusingly.

"She knows, doesn't she? I asked you not to tell her."

"It's way too late for that, Lindsay," I said, and poured the tea. "Mum?"

Mum drew a small white business card from her bag. "We're all in this together, now, Lindsay," she said. "You're much too precious for us to lose."

Lindsay stood shamefaced in the middle of the kitchen, hanging her head as if she'd just been caught out in some misdemeanour. She looked about ten. Mum got out of her chair and hugged Lindsay as tightly as she could, then both of them started crying. Whatever heart to heart they were going to have, I didn't think I should be getting in the way. I picked up my mug and slipped out of the room. I don't think either of them noticed.

I kept pretty much out of the way for the rest of the evening, but when I popped my head round the living-room door to say goodnight, Lindsay was in bed and Mum and Dad were watching *Newsnight*. Or rather, pretending to watch it.

"Everything all right?" I asked.

I don't know what I'd imagined, but Mum and Dad seemed remarkably cheerful under the circumstances.

"Ah, Chloe. Come in and sit down. Your mum was telling me just how well you sorted Lindsay out earlier."

I shrugged, wishing that the earth would swallow me up. I wasn't used to Dad being such a Mr Nice Guy.

"How is she?" I asked.

"Well, she actually ate a little bit of toast earlier," Mum said.

"And that digestive biscuit before," Dad reminded her. They could almost have been talking about an ailing grandparent.

"Good," I said. "It's a start."

They both nodded in unison, clearly wary of appearing too confident.

"And she's agreed to come and see the counsellor with us tomorrow," Mum said.

"That's great, too."

Dad put his hand over Mum's and squeezed it affectionately. "We're in this together, love, remember that. And together we'll get it beat."

There was something about the way he said it

that made me pretty certain that Lindsay was going to get better, however long it took. I climbed the stairs and started to get ready for bed. A feeling of drowsy contentment passed over me. It was my final exam tomorrow, I was going to be inundated with modelling jobs thereafter and make pots of money – who knows, maybe even enough to be able to pay rent on a share of a flat in London. Lindsay was showing all the signs of wanting to get free of her eating disorder by eating her first food in days. I prayed that this time, she wasn't trying to fool us like she did before.

When I received a letter from Greg the following day, which promised a romantic holiday for both of us beginning the very next week and containing an airline ticket for Corsica, I thought things couldn't get any better.

chapter thirty-five

Corsica, Mediterranean France. *L'ile de beauté* – the island of beauty. Endless sandy beaches and azure seas, spectacular sunsets and breathtaking coastal scenery, and Greg and me, alone at last. Idyllic, or what?

The first obstacle was Mum and Dad. OK, I was eighteen, and I wasn't asking them for money, I'd finished my exams and I was a free agent. Theoretically, I could just have said, *Right, that's me, I'm off*. And I would have done, had I been intending to spend the holiday with a bunch of girlfriends.

Thinking of girlfriends made me wonder if Kelly had already gone off to Greece with her new chums, and that brought me round to thinking about just how little I thought of her these days and how it bothered me even less.

I guess I finally knew that Kelly and I were officially no longer friends the day we walked past each other one afternoon, as we were both making our way to various exams, without even a hello. Instead of feeling unhappy about it, I actually felt relieved. Seemed that finally we could both stop pretending we mattered to each other.

But to get back to the subject of going on holiday with Greg. Sharing a holiday with him meant sharing a bed with him, which obvious fact I'm certain Dad would have picked up pretty quickly. Thing was, I was embarrassed to broach the topic — because I knew he'd be embarrassed. Should I leave it up to Mum to break the news that his innocent daughter was no longer the virgin he'd assumed she was all this time, I wondered.

Then there was Lindsay. I felt a bit guilty leaving her in the lurch like that after promising I'd be around for her as long as she needed me. I decided I'd talk to her first, tell her about my invitation and see what came out of it.

She was pretty definite. "For God's sake, Chloe,

go for it. You've just done your A levels. If anybody needs a break, you do. But if you don't fancy it, can I go in your place?"

So that was all right then. Mum was the next person to approach and why on earth I'd anticipated she would be an obstacle, I can't imagine.

"I think it sounds great," she said. She almost sounded relieved.

"But don't you need me around to police Lindsay? Be here when you and Dad are at work, that sort of thing?" I asked, wondering how soon it would be before she realized this herself.

"It's sweet of you, Chloe," Mum said. "Only I've actually decided to take some leave myself for the last three weeks of term. And most of Dad's teaching's finished now, too. Actually, we thought we'd take Linds out of school and go off to France ourselves. Nowhere as glamorous as where you're going though – probably Brittany."

"Ah, Brittany in the rain. Such fond memories," I joked.

Mum laughed. "Jealousy will get you nowhere," she said. "Actually, you going off like this will solve the problem of not having to ask you along."

"Don't worry, I know when I'm not wanted."

"No, don't take offence, Chloe," Mum said, although I hadn't at all. I'd already guessed that Mum and Dad were going to need some quality time with Lindsay if they were to help her overcome her problem.

"It's not that you'd get in the way or anything," Mum reassured me. "It's just that – well – if you're not here then Lindsay won't be comparing herself to you all the time."

"Is that what she does?" I was shocked. Then I thought about all the years I compared myself to Kelly, and always unfavourably. With a bit of imagination it wasn't so hard to get my head round.

"Lindsay has to learn that she's as worthy as the next person, the counsellor has told us. She needs to be at the centre of our lives right now. All our attention must be lavished on her twenty-four seven. Might be a bit hard when every time the phone rings it's your agent or your glamorous boyfriend."

I pondered this, then said: "You don't think I've been showing off a bit too much, do you Mum?"

Mum smiled. "A bit," she said. "But nobody would blame you. Trouble is, I've been showing off about you too. And Lindsay must have picked that up. She's not stupid."

She must have seen how uncomfortable I was looking, because she said, "None of Lindsay's illness is your fault, Chloe, so you must never think that."

"What caused it then," I wanted to know, "if it wasn't me?"

"If they knew that then curing those who suffer from it would be easy," she sighed. "Maybe it's just nature. You're either prone to it or not. Lindsay's always been a thoughtful child. Maybe that's a lot to do with it."

"She will get better, though, won't she?"

"Oh, absolutely," Mum said, with so much enthusiasm that I wasn't sure if I believed her. I said as much.

"You're not a child, Chloe. So I'm going to tell you exactly what I've been told." She drew a deep breath and went on. "The fact that you didn't believe Lindsay when she said that she'd stopped dieting – well, you'll never know just how grateful Dad and I are for your sharp eyes."

I was embarrassed but pleased at the same time. "The school was on to her too, remember?" I said.

"And they're doing everything they can to support her too," Mum added. "But it won't be easy. Getting Lindsay into a position where she feels comfortable around food and confident about her body weight isn't going to be straightforward. According to the counsellor it's quite likely to be two steps forward and one step back. And even if we manage to conquer it now, there's no guarantee she won't succumb again in the future. She'll need to be watched for a long time."

"Just like any addict," I said.

Mum nodded. "I'll never forgive myself for allowing myself to be taken in so easily. . ."

I interrupted with a stern, "Nonsense! She fooled me too, for ages. Turned deception into a fine art. If I'd not been off my food myself I wouldn't have noticed either."

It occurred to me that if Mum was to keep strong for Lindsay over the next few weeks or months, or however long it took to cure her, then she mustn't be allowed to blame herself or suffer self-reproach for any action she'd taken or failed to take in the past.

"You're a good girl, Chloe. I'll try to keep off the guilt trips in future. The counsellor's told us it's the worst thing I can do for myself. Thanks for reminding me."

A door banged shut behind us and we both gave a start. The last thing either of us wanted to be caught doing was scheming about Lindsay — and I'm sure that's exactly how she'd have interpreted it if she'd walked in and we'd both immediately stopped talking. With huge presence of mind, Mum immediately changed the subject.

"So about this holiday, then, Chloe? When d'you fly off?"

"I have a week to shop and pack and get my legs waxed," I said.

Then it's Greg and me alone on a magical island, having glorious sex, I didn't add.

chapter thirty-six

Excuse me, but did I say ALONE?

When I arrived at the airport in the car that had been sent to meet me, I was ushered into the VIP Lounge. *I could get used to this*, I thought, as my bags were whisked away and I scanned the other passengers for Greg. It was with a sinking heart that I picked out Jake, the only other band member whose name I could be sure of, leaning over someone who looked suspiciously like Tillie and lighting her fag for her.

What on earth was she doing here? Surely she wasn't travelling to the same place we were? It was too much of a coincidence! The thought of spending the next week avoiding her, or worse still being confronted by her in one of her drug-fuelled rages, was enough to make me wish I'd thought again before agreeing to come along. Well, Greg and I would just have to keep out of her way. We'd be staying in our luxury villa, anyway, as Greg had informed me in the note that had accompanied my flight ticket. From there — my idea — we'd visit all the places I'd spotted in the guidebook I'd rushed out to buy as soon as I knew I'd be visiting Corsica. We need never have to acknowledge Tillie at all, I decided.

I'd just about managed to come to terms with having to put up with Tillie's presence on the flight, when my eye alighted on three other vaguely familiar figures. At first I thought I must have been mistaken, but no, it was no mistake. This was no solitary love nest Greg and I would be holed up in. This was big time rock 'n' roll chillin' with anyone and everyone who had anything remotely to do with the band.

The other three members of Tough Love were joking with three girls I'd never set eyes on before. Over in a corner, a fat cigar in his podgy fingers, Tough Love's manager, Buzz Longhi — whom I'd only ever been briefly introduced to — lolled deep in conversation with a brassy Botox blonde who looked like she might self combust, she was dripping with so much gold. They were surrounded by a gaggle of children who seemed to be competing with each other to make the most amount of noise.

This was a nightmare! Other semi-familiar faces, assorted roadies and engineers and their various girlfriends, wives and children milled around in the general hubbub, exchanging conversation, checking watches, riffling through travel documents. I even thought I caught sight of Rob McGrath. What was this – Freeloaders Incorporated? Although, strictly speaking, no one as yet had asked me to put my hand in my pocket, so I don't suppose I was in any position to cast aspersions. The only things I'd had to cough up for had been my fortnight's supply of sexy underwear and assorted swimwear.

Why hadn't Greg mentioned that we'd be sharing our romantic hideaway with everyone on Buzz Longhi's payroll, apart from – maybe – the tea boy's granny?

Then I saw Greg at the door of the men's room, in his sexy shades with his jacket collar turned up. He looked every inch the glamorous rock star. I was about to call out to him, but decided it wouldn't be such a good idea. Greg was pretty hot these days. The last thing I wanted was to draw attention to him. Besides, if I was going to be sharing him on this holiday, I wanted him all to myself for now. I stalked him with my eyes, watching him make his way over to the café, head still down, but sneaking an occasional look around. I watched him take a seat and order something to drink from a hovering waiter and then I struck. Doing my best to remain unseen, I crept up behind him and removed his shades.

"Boo!" I shouted.

"Jesus Christ! What the hell do you think you're doing?" Greg snatched his shades back. "Don't you know this place is crawling with paparazzi? I haven't shaved this morning yet."

I opened my mouth in surprise and then immediately closed it again.

"So-*rry*. I wanted to surprise you. Aren't you pleased to see me?"

The waiter reappeared with Greg's bottle of water, his staple drink, and a glass, which he proceeded to set out on the table. Greg slammed his shades back on, but not before I'd glimpsed the dark shadows beneath his eyes and the pallor beneath the stubble.

"Well, you surprised me all right," he said.

Angry tears stung my eyes and I blinked them away.

Greg must have twigged that he'd upset me because he patted the seat next to him and said: "S'OK. Come and sit down. You're late."

I was about to say that actually I'd been here ages just hanging around and people-watching, but Greg jumped in with, "Get the lady a coffee," to the waiter who was still hovering by the table.

"Please," I reminded him. He shrugged, as if to acknowledge that of course he meant please, he'd just forgotten to say it was all.

"You haven't been getting your beauty sleep," I said. "Seems to have played havoc with your manners."

I'd heard of uppity pop stars losing touch with reality and thinking they need pay no attention to the rules of politeness that the rest of the world had to live with. Perhaps Greg had always been rude to people he didn't think important, only I'd never noticed before.

"I blame that on having to smile at fans and be

polite to stupid journalists, Chloe. It's a killer," he said. He suddenly brightened up. "You've been getting plenty of beauty sleep, though, that's easy to see. And a tan, too."

It wasn't enough for his magic to begin to weave its spell, though. I still had things to say about the other guys it looked like we'd be sharing our holiday with.

"It's as much a surprise to me as it is you," he said. It was impossible to read his eyes behind his shades, but I still thought he looked shifty.

"You said something about just the two of us," I said. "Looks like I misunderstood."

"Honest, Chloe, that's what I thought it was. I had no idea Buzz had invited all these other guys too. He's got his own villa on the island. Huge. Fifteen bedrooms." He lowered his voice. "It won't be so bad. We don't need to see anyone else all day, if we don't want to," he said, a cajoling note in his voice.

But I still wasn't finished with him. "And how do you explain Tillie?" I asked him, haughtily.

He groaned. "Don't ask me to. I can't," he said. "I haven't even spoken to her and don't intend to. As far as I know she's with the other guys."

"What? All of them?"

"I wouldn't be surprised," he said. "I told you. I've kept as far away from her as possible since she assaulted me."

"Well, just as long as she keeps out of my way," I said.

"She will. So, am I forgiven?"

"I suppose so," I said. I was beginning to be seduced by the teasing note in his voice. He removed his shades and edged closer. He had this way of looking at me that shot me through with a longing for him that was impossible to hide. Moving ever closer, he tilted my face upwards and suddenly we were kissing as if we were going for a gold medal.

"Mmmm," he murmured, as we finally prised our mouths apart. "That was worth the wait."

What is it about the promise of sex that makes us feel we are in love? Up until the moment he touched me and rekindled the spark of desire that was even now spreading a flame throughout my body, I'd been starting to question my feelings about Greg. This morning he'd shown himself to be arrogant and rude. I'd even been almost ready to believe he'd lied to me and knew all along that we wouldn't be alone on holiday. But now, after that kiss, his arm slung casually around my shoulder, our heads, thighs and knees touching as we sat and waited for our flight to be called, I was totally and utterly his.

OK, so the housing arrangements weren't exactly what I'd anticipated but it would have been churlish of me to admit to a twinge of disappointment that Greg and I weren't going to be marooned somewhere on our own.

So a fifteen-bedroom villa with your own maid and two swimming pools to choose from plus your own private strip of beach ain't good enough no more? *Get a grip, girl*, I told myself. Perhaps I was letting this celebrity stuff go to my head more than Greg was – and I wasn't even a celebrity!

I thought of Mum and Dad and Lindsay in some muddy field in France, wondering when they could get their next hot bath. By comparison I had absolutely nothing to complain about. This was going to be a holiday of a lifetime, and I intended making the most of every moment.

chapter thirty-seven

The villa was like something you could only dream
of, located in a wide sweep of its very own private
bay where a yacht – presumably belonging to Buzz
Longhi – glinted white on the turquoise water. The
sand stretched for what seemed like miles, as clean
as only sand could be which was raked twice daily by
the hired hands. The walls of the villa were washed a
pastel pink, and, I was to discover, changed their hue
to deep red as the sun sank down and finally disappeared behind the horizon. Palm trees, their green
fronds dancing in the light, hot breeze, shaded two
kidney-shaped pools around which exotic plants I
couldn't name were casually but tastefully arranged,
lending their fragrance to the air.

The room allocated to Greg and me had its own en suite bathroom and view of the bay. We went there first to unpack. Drinks would be served on the terrace in half an hour, we were told, but the band members and some of their entourage wouldn't be coming along as they had a very important business meeting scheduled.

"Business meeting?" I wailed. Just as I'd got over my hissy fit about numbers, something else was getting in the way of the magic spell I'd conjured up for Greg and me. "But you're supposed to be on holiday!"

"Buzz doesn't know what the word means," Greg said. He was calling from the bathroom – door open – where he was finally getting round to having a shave. "That's why he's worth millions, I guess."

"But can't you just cry off? I want to go to the pool or just – well, stay here for a bit. I thought we could catch up. I've got loads to tell you and you slept all the way here."

Was I whining? From the look on Greg's face as he trailed out of the bathroom, he certainly felt so. I perched myself on the end of the king-size bed with its crisp white sheets and willed Greg to change his mind.

"No can do, babe. This is contract stuff. Megabucks. We've had an offer from a different label. He wants to explain the small print."

As he leaned down to plant a perfunctory kiss on my head I caught the scent of his aftershave. "Hey. We've got a fortnight of this. A half-hour meeting. An hour at the most. That's all I'm talking about. Then we can do whatever you want. Don't nag, Chloe, it doesn't become you," he said.

I felt as if he'd dealt me a fatal blow. Nag? Nag! I didn't nag. I was too young and cool and hip to nag. Nagging was what your mum did when you hadn't tidied your room like she'd asked. Your dad nagged about make-up and the length of your skirt. Your teacher nagged about coursework and the fact that the only person to do any work in the classroom was herself.

"I'm having a shower," I said, jumping up from the bed, with all the dignity I could muster. "Then I'm going for a swim."

"What about the drinks reception?"

"I'm on holiday, Greg," I said. "That means I get a drink when I want a drink, not when I'm summoned."

I grabbed my washbag, slammed the bathroom

door behind me and shot the bolt, my heart pumping fast. I turned on the shower full pelt and stood beneath it, finding some perverse enjoyment from being attacked by so many sharp needles of hot water. Greg might be expected to work, but I'd just finished my A levels, for Chrissake, and if other people were happy to be summoned for drinks on the terrace, that was fine by me. At least I'd get the pool to myself.

Or so I thought. As I approached the pool, the water rippled and someone's dark head appeared from beneath the surface, to the accompaniment of a great deal of spluttering and splashing.

"Hey! Chloe! Great to see you. Getting in? Or is the outfit just a fashion accessory?"

It was Rob McGrath, looking like a person who had found his true element. Droplets of water glistened on his eyelashes and his dark hair – which he'd clearly allowed to grow since the last time I'd seen him at close quarters – dripped in clumps on to his broad, already deeply tanned shoulders. He grinned up at me as he trod water and waited for me to decide what I wanted to do.

"I didn't think you'd be down here when there's all that free booze waiting for you on the terrace."

I pronounced the last syllable of the final word to sound like "arse" and Rob laughed.

"Not my style," he said. "Not yours either, from the sound of things."

I shrugged. I didn't want Rob picking up the fact that there might be bad vibes between Greg and me. He'd given me enough clues that he wasn't overly impressed with my choice of boyfriend in the past.

"Now, are you getting in or not? The water's terrific."

"Try stopping me," I said. Normally, I would have made my way wimpishly down the steps, clutching the rail on the way down, not being as confident in water as Rob clearly was. But the challenging look on his face made it clear he expected me to be the kind of swimmer who never ever got her face wet and I was determined to prove him wrong. Besides, I needed some kind of physical release. I was still smarting from Greg's insult. *Nag! I'll give him nag*, I muttered to myself grimly as I took a running jump and hurled myself into the water.

I came up coughing and spluttering, my eyes stinging and my throat on fire, but I felt triumphant. Gradually the chill of the water was replaced by the delicious feeling of warm sunlight on my back as I progressed the length of the pool by means of a ladylike breaststroke.

Rob and I didn't exchange any other conversation for the next half-hour apart from the occasional grunt of pleasure at the surroundings we found ourselves in, as we passed each other up and down the pool. After a while he hauled himself out of the water and made for his towel.

"Trust an Aussie, Chloe. You need to cover up round about now or you'll cook."

"Oh, I never burn," I said confidently, but all the same I followed him out of the water. The swim had been nice, but I'd had enough for now. My bad mood had abated with the exercise and put some kind of perspective on my row with Greg. Thinking about it from his point of view, maybe I had been nagging. After all, he hadn't been the one to call the meeting, and I'm sure, given a choice, he would have preferred to be here with me.

I scrambled into the wrap I'd brought with me and went to grab one of the sunbeds.

"So, how come you got an invite to this place, then?" I wanted to know. "I didn't think you knew any of this crowd." Then I figured it out. "Unless your Uncle Charlie came up trumps again."

Rob grinned. "Dead right," he said. "He did some photos of the band and they turned out so well their manager offered him a holiday. Only he couldn't make it because of work. And also because he can't stand Buzz Lightyear."

I made the smallest attempt not to snigger.

"What's wrong with him?" I asked. "Apart from his suits and his horrible cigars. Oh, and his family."

"Buzz Longhi is a control freak," Rob said. "Uncle Charlie would probably end up murdering him before too long."

"And what about you? Don't you mind being controlled?"

Rob shrugged. "I'm small fry," he said. "No one cares what I do, or where I go for that matter. But I guess it'll be different for you and Greg and the rest of the boys in the band."

I was beginning to feel a chill spread through me, even though the temperature must have been hitting the thirties. What was Rob suggesting?

"I should forget about you and Greg going off on your own to explore the island if what I've heard is true. Longhi likes lavish dinners here in the villa and trips out on the yacht, himself at the helm. Oh, and accompanied by whichever publication has paid the most to catch the stars in their unguarded moments. You know the kind of thing. 'A tanned and hunky Greg Geffen shares an intimate moment with his willowy model girlfriend Chloe Dove.'"

He lay back on his recliner and set his face towards the sun. "Although I guess Greg already told you all this stuff, and you figured as long as you were together it didn't matter?"

Was Rob fishing for information about just how much Greg told me, I wondered, or was he just being sarky? With that rising Australian intonation it was hard to tell. I sat in silence for some time, mulling over his words. I was pretty sure he'd guessed from my silence that this was the first I'd heard of any deal with a magazine. Was the whole thing just some huge publicity stunt, and had Greg been lying to me about this, too? My anger with him took hold again. Why had he felt the need to deceive me on so many counts?

I'd brought my guidebook. I wanted to visit the beauty spots – the Citadelle of Bonafacio, which I'd read was situated precariously on top of a headland of white limestone cliffs. The Pointe de la Parata –

a wild black granite headland famous for its spectacular sunsets. Both these places and more I wanted to share with Greg – not with a bunch of people I hardly knew, and certainly not with a photographer in tow.

I didn't want lavish dinners on the terrace, either. I wanted to eat the food the natives ate and I wanted to eat in the same places they did. I wanted to hear French all around me instead of English. I wanted to wander around narrow dusty streets with a map I couldn't read and sit at pavement cafés, with a glass of whatever was the natives' favourite tipple, soaking up the foreignness of it all.

Rob sat up again, and removed his shades, then peered at me, anxiously. "He didn't say anything to you, did he, about this?"

When I didn't reply he said. "Aw, me and my big mouth. Honest, Chloe, I didn't say all that stuff to put Greg in a bad light or anything. I kind of assumed he'd have told you and that you'd. . ."

"Spare me your convoluted logic, Rob. I know you don't like Greg and you enjoy showing him in a bad light, but sneaking to me behind his back like this is pitiful."

I waited for Rob to deny my accusation but he didn't, which made me even madder at him than I was at Greg. If I'd been able to think quicker on my feet I'd have said breezily that of course I'd known all along that the press would be here too, but the flight and the hot sun had made my brain about as quick on the uptake as a sloth's. I decided to try again, but even as I opened my mouth I knew I could only sound unconvincing at best and pompous at worst.

"It's clear why Greg didn't tell me any of this stuff," I said. "He cares for me and he wants to be with me however and whenever he can. It's not easy in this business to keep a relationship going. Greg is doing his best under the circumstances and I'm extremely grateful to him for considering my feelings and protecting me from the seedy business side of things and. . ."

Rob threw his hands in the air and interrupted me. "OK, fine," he yelled. "If that's what you want to believe, Chloe, then go ahead."

He leaped off his sunbed with such vigour that his shades flew off his face and into the water. It was so ridiculous that we both stopped being mad and grinned at each other foolishly.

"I guess I'd better retrieve them," he said and jumped in.

Somewhere in my peripheral vision I caught sight of people heading this way. Looked like drinkies were over and the photoshoot was about to begin. Nobody would want to photograph me with my hair plastered to my head and my mascara running, I figured. I jumped in the water after Rob.

chapter thirty-eight

Round the pool Greg was charm itself, waving at Rob — who didn't wave back — like he was his best buddy and asking me how the water was. Why was he being so friendly all of a sudden? Had he forgotten that I was a nag?

Just then I caught a glimpse of some creepy-looking guy in a baseball cap, with a beer gut he had no qualms about showing off to the rest of the assembled company. He had at least three cameras slung round his neck. So. That was Greg's game. He was being nice to me for the sake of the press. Poor deluded me. I decided the photographer was having not one single picture of me and ducked underwater to help Rob, who was still swimming around trying to locate his shades.

A few others were now dipping their toes cautiously in the water or — in the case of Buzz Longhi's children — throwing themselves in with noisy abandon. Tillie drifted over to the poolside, a dreamy expression on her face, like she was in some other world. She was ghastly white compared to everyone else in her one-piece black swimsuit, her face almost completely covered by a huge pair of shades. Her ash blonde hair looked lank, with its dark roots showing, scraped back from her elfin face unflatteringly. She looked fragile enough to snap in two.

Rob surfaced a couple of metres away from me, triumphantly clutching his retrieved shades. His expression changed immediately he saw Tillie.

"Swim over to the other end and help me keep Tillie out of the water," he said in an undertone. "I don't like the look of her."

I opened my mouth to ask him why on earth I should, but before I could think of a clever way of saying it, he said: "Please. If she's been drinking — or whatever — she shouldn't get in the water. Those louts should be looking after her but they're too busy having their pictures taken."

I looked over to where various members of the band were posing — tossing a beach ball about, laughing and joking and pushing each other playfully. There were a few girls hanging around too, although none risked getting wet until they'd been photographed looking lush and lovely, lipgloss and hair extensions still in place.

"Would you get a look at the arm candy?" Rob whistled.

I wished I could have found it as amusing as he did. But his choice of words disturbed me. Arm candy. That's exactly how I would have described them at one time, too. But if they were arm candy how was I any different? What if I were no more special than any of these other girls pouting at the camera and giggling like crazy whenever one of the boys said anything remotely amusing?

"Come on then, Mr Knight in Shining Armour," I snapped. "Let's go and rescue the fair damsel in distress."

I struck out for the other side of the pool, thinking to beat Rob to it, but I guess his Australian upbringing meant he'd probably learned to swim before he could walk. By the time I reached the other end of the pool and clambered out, Rob and

Tillie were deep into a conversation.

Tillie gave me a vacant grin. Clearly I was her best friend again. And clearly she was drugged to the eyeballs.

"I was just saying." Her speech was slurred, her posture slack. "Look at that photographer over there. If he can't make any money selling his photographs he can always go down to the beach and sell his shade."

She dissolved into hysterics at her own joke. Rob and I exchanged a look.

"Heard anything from Kendall?" Rob asked brightly. "Looks like she got her big break at last."

I pricked up my ears. It had been ages since I'd given Kendall any thought at all, or Sofia too, for that matter.

Tillie made some attempt to pull herself into an upright position and clapped her hands like a delighted child. "Oh, Rob, you're right! Can you imagine! Two weeks in Milan on the catwalk. She's doing all the major shows. Anybody who's everybody will be there." She clapped her hand over her beautiful mouth and giggled. "Or do I mean everybody who's anybody?"

"Well, if anyone deserves to become a

supermodel then Kendall certainly does," he said. "She's a stunner."

A rush of irritation shot through me. I was being irrational, I knew, but Rob's naked admiration of Kendall infuriated me. I resolved to keep quiet. It was nothing to do with me who Rob McGrath fancied. But Kendall!

"She's a real saint too," he added.

Tillie nodded in fervent agreement. I couldn't keep my resolve up any longer.

"Kendall? A saint?" I spluttered. "Like — how exactly? She's not entirely been forthcoming with the saintly behaviour whenever I've come into contact with her."

I think I showed remarkable restraint when I failed to add that as far as I was concerned she was one poisonous bitch. Call me quick to catch on, but from the look on Rob's face, I reckon if I'd uttered one more word against her then he would have struck me dead on the spot.

"Kendall's mother's dying from multiple sclerosis," he said. "She has a kid brother who needs a lot of emotional support. The dad walked out years ago. Kendall supports the family single-handedly. Looks after her mother every day she's not working, always on the end of the phone for her brother. Yeah, I guess she's pretty much a saint."

Suddenly I felt like a louse and Rob knew it.

"Hey, don't worry about it, Chloe," he said. "You weren't to know. Kendall's not the type to blow her own trumpet so why would you?"

"No. Well. Even so," I stammered, unable to look him in the eye I was so embarrassed.

It was a relief when Tillie began one more fit of the hysterics.

"Oh God, would you just look at Greg," she giggled.

Rob and I turned our heads simultaneously in Greg's direction.

"Sure knows how to strike a pose," Tillie went on. "S'almost uncanny the way he seems to sense that the camera's pointing his way and holds it for just the right amount of time, isn't it?"

"Steady, Tillie." This time Rob was on my side. "Be careful what you say. Remember Chloe's here."

I wasn't going to get into a cat fight with Tillie. I followed Greg's progress as he strolled around the pool alone, deep in thought, hands in his jeans pockets. He was somehow distanced from the hilarity – forced or otherwise – that everyone else was indulging in.

It was exactly that aloof manner, the way he had of somehow disconnecting himself from those around him, that I'd found so attractive when I'd first seen him the day of the video shoot. Catching him in the same pose at the airport earlier in the day had rekindled the image of him I'd been carrying around my head through all the intervening weeks of our separation. I remember thinking he must have been looking for me. But what if he was just striking that pose for any paparazzi that happened to be lurking in the vicinity?

Right now, he seemed to be on another planet. A casual observer might think he was writing a song in his head, and walking round the pool like that, occasionally pausing to look up at the sky, or crouching to run the water through his fingers was helping him get some inspiration. Not Tillie, though.

"Look where the photographer is," Tillie hissed. "Not that Greg can possibly have spotted him, of course!"

I spun round and spied the fat photographer – now burnt red from the sun – squatting behind a palm tree, clearly in Greg's line of vision. Tillie had been the first to spot that Greg knew perfectly well he was being photographed. I could have laughed her observation off as sour grapes on her part. But the thing was – I knew she was right. Greg's behaviour was nothing more than play-acting – a ploy to draw the camera away from anyone else who might have been fancying a bit of limelight, keeping it fully trained on himself.

In books, when such a revelation occurs, a cloud passes in front of the sun, a cool breeze causes our heroine to shiver and the first drops of rain that will soon become a deluge start to fall. But, hey. This was Corsica in July. And if anything it was getting hotter.

Without saying a word to either Tillie or Rob, I scrambled up from the side of the pool, feeling slightly sick from the revelation Tillie had given me, and headed for the villa – which unfortunately meant passing Greg. As I approached he looked at me almost as if he hated me.

"You look like a drowned rat," he hissed. "I'm coming back with you. I think we need to get one or two things sorted out."

I smiled sweetly at him, just in case the camera

was still pointing this way. "Fine," I said. "If that's what you want."

So that was row number two. Or was it three? Or maybe even four? I'd lost count. Everything I did seemed to irritate Greg. Back in the bedroom he demanded to know what I'd been doing mucking about in the water with Rob when I should have been making myself beautiful for the camera?

I reminded him that just as he'd failed to inform me we were sharing this villa with anyone who'd ever been on Buzz Longhi's payroll, so he'd omitted to make it clear that I was expected to be on public display for the next two weeks.

"How can you think I want to come away on holiday with a photographer, Greg? I came to be with you. Besides, I'm a model. If I pose I get paid. It's a job."

The sudden switch in Greg's mood from waspish irritation to that of a humble chastened child made me suspicious. He came over to where I was shivering on the bed, sat down next to me and put his arm around my shoulder.

I suppressed the urge to shrug it off, and let it remain, but my initial instinct to recoil left me feeling uncomfortable and depressed. Just yesterday the thought that I might ever find Greg so unattractive that I didn't want him near me would have been ludicrous. How could you be in love with a person one moment and then hate them so finally and irrevocably the next?

"Chloe, baby. I know why you're mad at me. You think I'm neglecting you, don't you?" He removed his arm from my shoulder and took my two hands between his. "Look at me now. I'm right, aren't I?"

The thing about Greg's eyes – I may have said it before – they were by far his best feature. Once you'd looked into them, there was no way you could drag your own away. His eyes were the core of his charisma – and in this moment, he was exploiting the sexual magnetism they projected as fully as he was able to.

I wanted to say that it wasn't that he was neglecting me that had upset me at all, but the fact that he'd lied to me. But now it was impossible. Much easier, I decided – only I didn't decide, his penetrating eyes decided for me – to go along with his assumption. I may have given an imperceptible nod, just enough to acknowledge that there was a bit of truth in his assumption, but it certainly wasn't the whole truth. It was enough, however, for Greg to assume he had the go-ahead to make love to me.

I wish I could have said that I wasn't able to enjoy sex with Greg this time, not while I was in the middle of working out just exactly how I felt about him, now my illusions had fallen away. Only it would have been a lie. For both of us, I'm convinced, this was the best time ever. But afterwards, as we lay apart on the bed, I was gripped by the certainty that what I felt for Greg was not and never had been love at all, but sheer physical lust.

How could I love him, after all? I knew so little about him, for one thing. What did we talk about when we were together? For the most part, like now, Greg discouraged talk. There was too much talking in the world, he maintained, too much analysing how you felt. That's why he sang songs, he would joke.

But words mattered to me. Unless I talked I didn't know how I felt. Was that crazy? Maybe. With Greg, the talking never got any bigger than small. And whereas in the beginning I'd been charmed by this and convinced myself that the sparing way he used words hinted at hidden depths, I think that maybe I'd suspected all along that there was very little going on in Greg Geffen's ahead beside Greg Geffen. Those silences on the phone whenever I'd changed the subject from modelling to college, the way I'd never felt able to open up to him about Lindsay, like I guessed he'd just shrug my feelings away as being trivial. His recent performance at the pool was just one more factor. And what he said next confirmed my certainty that I'd been a complete idiot ever to allow myself to be so easily taken in.

"Buzz was saying at the meeting that you and I should get engaged."

I was incapable right then of processing Greg's words. It was as if my brain had turned into thick, gloopy mud. All I could do was hang on in disbelief, while his words grappled to find a footing. When they finally stumbled, sinking without trace, it was a relief. Now I would never even have to acknowledge they'd been spoken.

Somewhere in the back of my mind I remembered the suggestion Kendall had made that if I looked good enough, Greg might ask me to marry him. Greg was serious. He was not only serious, he was crazy.

"So what do you think?" he said.

chapter thirty-nine

Somehow I managed to haul myself up off the bed and propel myself to the bathroom where I spent the next fifteen minutes under the shower. I hated myself for allowing myself to be seduced so easily, and I felt dirty. I wanted to go home. Or rather I wanted to be anywhere but here. For the second time that day I let the water shoot off me in powerful jets and tried to stop my ears to the memory of Greg's words. But it was no use. They wouldn't be silenced.

I could do three things, I decided, as I dried myself off and slathered my skin with after-sun. I could walk back in and pretend our last encounter had never happened. If Greg were foolish enough to bring the subject up again, I could just widen my eyes and tell him that naturally I'd thought it was a joke. Funny – but not that funny. Then I could pack my bags, and sneak away on the next available flight back to England.

Or I could walk back in and have the most enormous row with Greg and finish our relationship in a more dramatic way. How could he imagine I would consider getting engaged to him just because his manager thought it might be a good idea? Even if it hadn't been his idea, couldn't he at least have pretended it was? What female, however besotted she was, could possibly accept a proposal because a third party had *thought it was a good idea*! Besides, he needed to know that I was no longer besotted. Maybe I'd even enjoy telling him that, actually, I was beginning to despise him.

But it was the third thing I chose to do. There was a timid knock at the bathroom door. Clearly, Greg wasn't so insensitive that he hadn't grasped I might be hopping mad, then? Well, that was something.

"Chloe. Dinner's being served in half an hour. I'm going for a dip to cool off and I'll see you down there, OK?"

I marvelled at his cool.

"The fuck you will," I muttered beneath my breath. I wasn't staying here to eat, that was for sure. Not with Buzz Longhi looking fondly across the table at me like I was some prospective daughter-in-law and asking if we'd named the day yet.

Gingerly, I stuck my head round the bathroom door. No sign of Greg. I grabbed a white silk shift dress from the rail and slipped it over my head, slid my brown feet into my highest heels and gave my hair a cursory brushing. A quick check on my reflection reassured me that all I needed to offset my tan was a slick of lipgloss and I'd be ready to hit the town.

But wait a minute. Who the hell was I going to hit the town with? I stepped out on to the balcony. The air was cooler now – more pleasant – and the sun cast long shadows over the view. There didn't seem to be anyone about at all. Presumably, once Buzz Longhi summoned you to eat, you made pretty damn sure you were hungry.

There *was* one person down there, though, I realized, as my eyes became accustomed to the dazzle from the sun's sinking rays, and it wasn't

Greg. Dressed in a white T-shirt and sandals and wearing cut-off jeans which might have sported a designer label but were more likely just to be an old pair gone at the knees and recycled, Rob, completely absorbed in his task, was taking photographs of the sunset. So, he was skiving too — and, like me, not for the first time that day. I decided to hijack him.

"Hey, Rob," I called out and watched his confusion as he tried to locate where the voice was coming from. "I'm up here. On the balcony. To your left."

He peered upwards until he saw me and as I waved he quickly put his camera to his face and snapped my picture. I laughed, not at all irritated by what he'd done.

"It'll cost you," I called out. "My rates are astronomical these days."

"Tell me the damage, then." He spoke good-naturedly.

"Dinner."

He pondered for a while, then turned out his pockets.

"No tengo dinero."

"Wrong language," I laughed.

"Well, whatever language you choose I'm still skint in it. Look, I'm getting a crick in my neck. Quit with the Juliet stuff and come down."

On impulse I decided to exchange my stilettos for flip-flops. If I was going to spend the evening with a beach bum, then I might just possibly get away with my dress. The shoes, however, were a definite no-no.

"So why aren't you with — everyone else?"

Was it my imagination, or was Rob avoiding mentioning Greg by name? As soon as he asked me I realized I should have thought up some reason for not being with Greg. But what could I say? The truth? That I'd been an idiot and fallen for a guy who thought he was the centre of the universe? I groped towards a sort of explanation and prayed it would be convincing enough. I still had *some* self-esteem left, though Greg might not have thought so from the way I'd just thrown myself at him.

"It's been a long day. I didn't fancy a crowd and I had a bit of a headache. I told Greg to go to dinner without me and then I fell asleep. I'm not sure I've got the nerve to walk in now. What if they're in the middle of their first course?"

Rob didn't take his eyes off me throughout my entire explanation.

"You're lying, Chloe, but it's none of my business," he said. "Good job for you I'm not a tabloid journalist. Come on, let's get going if you're hungry. I'm starving!"

Rob strode off towards the gates and I followed quickly behind, casting my eyes about me furtively as we left the villa behind us. I was anxious to be far away and out of sight. Not that I had anything to feel guilty about. What did I care about what a bunch of people I didn't even know thought?

We were heading away from our more-or-less secluded, private area of beach towards a busier stretch of the little coastal town now. Beautifully-dressed couples paraded by, cars honked their horns, the air was filled with the sound of music and laughter. It was getting dark and coloured lights twinkled through the leaves of the palm trees, adding to the festive feel. It was impossible to resist being caught up in the atmosphere and part of the throng. Damn it! I was on holiday, wasn't I? Why should I resist? Corsica had to be one of the most beautiful places I'd ever visited in my life. I was going to have fun while I could, I decided. If Buzz Longhi chucked me out of his villa for upsetting one of his protégés, then too bad.

"I read the food here is great," Rob said.

"I read that too," I said. "More Italian than French."

"Guess you've got the same guide as me," he said, pulling a dog-eared duplicate of my much smarter one from the back pocket of his jeans.

We grinned at each other. "Fancy a quick pizza?" I said.

"You bet."

There were so many interesting-looking restaurants that we couldn't settle on one. For a while we paraded back and forth along the promenade, stopping at each eating place, reading the menu, then moving on to the next, on the off chance it was better.

"Hey, this is silly," Rob said, after about twenty minutes of this dithering. "If we wait any longer we'll die of starvation."

Finally we settled on the restaurant we'd both fancied in the first place and waited to be seated. A quick pizza we'd agreed to. But this was France. Where people thought fast food referred to how long it took a meal to be prepared, not how long it took the diners to eat it. Half an hour stretched to an hour and one hour stretched to two. By the time we'd consumed our pizza, drunk a couple of beers and then a bottle of red wine, I guess we just lost track of time. Rob was a great talker. He'd travelled all over the world – lived to travel, so he said – and throughout our meal he regaled me with traveller's tales.

"You've got to tell me to shut up if I'm boring you," he said, breaking off in the middle of a description of the toilet arrangements in a hostel he'd once stayed in somewhere in South Africa.

I shook my head fervently. "If I'm yawning it's just because I had to get up so early and – well – it's been a bit of an eventful day."

It was hard to believe, actually, that it was still the same day that had begun when my alarm clock had gone off at 4.30 this morning to make sure I got to the airport in time.

"What about an ice cream?" Rob said. As soon as I hinted that I might be on the point of bringing up Greg in the conversation, he changed the subject.

"This ice cream is the stuff they serve in heaven, I'm convinced," I said later, as I ploughed my way through a mound of pistachio and velvety vanilla.

"Good to see you eat," Rob said. "Most girls these days seem to exist on a cotton-wool ball soaked in water and a pot of lipgloss every few days."

I found myself telling Rob about Lindsay then, and about my concerns for her.

"I could kick myself for not realizing there was something going on with her sooner," I said, towards the end of my tale. "Things are going to take so much longer to put right now. If they ever can be."

Rob touched my hand tentatively and said: "They will be. You've just got to keep her in your sight. Don't trust her, but don't let her know you don't. Anorexics are like junkies. They'll lie to you all the time about what they've eaten."

"Sounds like you have some experience."

The coffee arrived and as we drank it Rob told me about his older sister Lucy, who'd had all sorts of problems round food for years, right from being about eleven or twelve.

"Course I was too little to understand what was going on back then, being nine years her junior. But as I grew older, well. . ." He shook his head and a look of pain crossed his face. "The worst bit was when we visited her in hospital. She had all sorts of wires poking out of her. At that point she weighed about five stone. The girl she was sharing a room with in hospital had died the previous week."

He must have seen my look of panic and guessed I was imagining Lindsay in the same position, because he immediately reassured me that Lucy had recovered, although it had taken years before she was able to feel really at ease around food, and she was living a normal life now. He fiddled in his wallet and drew out a picture.

"In fact, look. This is her."

The picture showed a perfectly normal-sized woman, with Rob's broad shoulders, dark hair and deep tan, smiling at the camera. She was holding hands with a little blonde girl who couldn't have been more than four or five. The little girl was beaming and waving at the camera. I gave Rob an enquiring look.

"My niece," he said. "Emma. I'm completely crazy about her. Don't get me on to the subject of Emma, though, or we'll be here till midnight."

He put the precious picture away quickly, but he wasn't quick enough for me not to notice the look of intense pride he gave it first.

"You know, you're a really nice bloke, do you mind if I say that?" I think I was a bit drunk and a lot tired, otherwise, I swear, I would never have allowed such a corny remark to pass my lips.

"You're not so bad yourself." Rob looked suddenly shy and I felt dreadful for patronizing him like that.

"Why do you dislike Greg so much, Rob?" There, now I'd asked him the question I'd wanted to ask all night.

Rob looked evasive. "Look, Chloe, I . . . He's your fella. I'm not gonna slag him off in front of you, am I?"

"Thing is, Rob. Actually I don't think he is my fella – my boyfriend – any more."

"Oh? Since when?"

I shrugged. "Since we got here. Since he revealed just how shallow he was. All that posing round the pool. All that sucking up to Buzz Longhi. And something you said about arm candy. That's all I am to Greg and that's all I've ever been. Only until today I was too naïve to get it."

Rob made a sound of protest but I held up my hand to silence him.

"No, Rob. Don't start getting all diplomatic

again. There's no need. I'm cool about it."

The people at the next table were leaving, and as one of the women went to reach for the wrap she'd draped over the back of her chair I managed to catch a glimpse of her wristwatch.

"Sh-it!"

"What?"

"When you said, just then, that we'd be here till midnight — well, actually, you're five minutes out. It's five-past."

chapter forty

Hurriedly we got the bill and argued about who was going to pay. Rob found some Euros and insisted he was repaying a debt, reminding me how I'd demanded payment earlier in the evening. It was clearly a matter of pride with him, so I decided not to argue. I decided that next time we went out it would be my treat and then I checked myself. What did I mean next time? There would be no next time. I was going home as soon as I could book a return flight.

But first, I had to negotiate Greg and tell him we were through. Walking back, Rob and I barely spoke, but concentrated on putting one foot in front of the other, grateful for the coffee buzz that made walking just about possible.

We were in the grounds of the villa now, and it was eerily quiet. Somewhere someone was laughing and music drifted through the air, but apart from that — nothing. I shivered, although it was a warm night.

"You OK?"

"I half-expected an armed gunman on the gate," I said. "Or at least a couple of rottweilers sniffing for escaped prisoners."

Rob chuckled. "I know what you mean," he said. "You have to keep reminding yourself this is a holiday home and not a prison camp."

"I think I'll go straight up if it's OK with you. I'm bushed."

Someone must have seen us arrive because the main door clicked open to admit us, just as the gates had done. So much for my theory that security was minimal here. Not minimal, clearly — just so sophisticated you didn't notice it.

"If there's any trouble, Chloe, I was the one who insisted we had something to eat, remember."

"Thanks, Rob. You're a good mate."

"Yeah. And a really nice bloke. Like you said. Night, Chloe."

He gave me a lazy wave then climbed the steps two at a time. I stood watching him until he disappeared from view, wishing I didn't have to step over the threshold to my room and face Greg again. What would I do? Allow him to bring up the subject of an engagement again, or just grab my things and make a dash for it?

He was asleep, or so I thought as I clicked open the door as quietly as I could. But the alacrity with which he snapped on the bedside lamp as soon as I closed the door behind me was proof that he'd simply been lying there in the dark, waiting for my return.

I'd kind of expected him to be mad with me at disappearing without even leaving him a message. In my head I'd already counted the different ways he could show his displeasure. I'd bargained for cold, righteous anger. How dare I just walk off like that with another guy? Did I have any idea how hurtful my actions had been? I'd bargained for silence – a bristling resentment that no amount of explanation would be able to penetrate. I'd even bargained for him flying into a rage. What would I do if he got violent, I wondered.

But what I hadn't bargained for was what actually occurred.

"You're back safe then? Not that anyone thought you wouldn't be. Buzz had a tail on you."

I was so knackered I was pretty sure that I'd just heard Greg tell me he'd had me tailed. Surely I was hallucinating?

"Come on, then. Get into bed." He patted the pillow next to him.

I was rooted to the spot. Was Greg playing some sick joke on me? Was this an example of the playful sense of humour all those pre-teen magazines insisted he had? Did he seriously think I was going to get into bed with him? I'd come for my stuff, that was all. I'd sleep on a recliner round the pool sooner than sleep with him.

Greg smiled at me benignly. "Don't look at me like that, Chloe. I'm not angry with you. I asked you to get engaged. It's a big step. You needed to talk it over with a mate. I don't approve of your choice, but then I suspect the kangaroo isn't my biggest fan either. Slag me off, did he?"

"Rob didn't say a word about you. Neither of us mentioned you at all, actually. We spent the evening eating pizza and ice cream and talking about other stuff."

Greg's brow furrowed. Clearly this was the

wrong thing to say.

"Greg, for God's sake, I thought you were just having a laugh. I'm eighteen, for God's sake. Why would I want to get engaged?"

"In general, do you mean, or to me in particular?"

I didn't want to answer, but I was pretty sure my face said it all.

He peered out in the half-light, his mouth turned down in a sulk and his arms crossed against his chest.

"It was Buzz's idea, you know. Not mine. He thought you were the right type for me. It's easy to get the wrong kind of girlfriend in this business."

It's funny, but when you fall out of love with someone, everything about them immediately becomes repugnant to you. Greg's voice — which I'd always considered to be his next best feature — tinged as it was with an edge of croaky fatigue that once sent shivers down my spine, now came over as a petulant whine. His slit of a mouth, that earlier today roused me to heights of passion, repulsed me now. But if all those things provoked such strong loathing in me, what he said sent me reeling with fury.

"You're seriously telling me you had me vetted before you asked me out?"

"Well, not in so many words. But things had gone a bit pear-shaped with that Tillie. Like I told you. Buzz didn't want a repetition."

I was stupefied with exhaustion, desperate to lie down and close my eyes. My ears rang with the surging blood of my rage and my temples throbbed to its beat.

"You seriously expect me to get into that bed with you and stay with you for the rest of this holiday after you've told me that?"

He threw back the duvet and, naked, swung his legs over the side of the bed. "All things considered, probably not. I'll bed down with one of the lads, if any of them are on their own. Or even if they're not. It'll be quite like old times."

"Wait."

Greg was pulling on some clothes. He stopped with his pants halfway up his legs. From the lascivious look on his face, he clearly thought I'd changed my mind. I glared at him, throwing a look of disgust at his white butt, marched over to a drawer where I kept my passport and the money I'd brought and grabbed my chequebook and a pen.

"I don't know how much my ticket cost, but take this. It's all the money I've earned from the jobs I've done. I've never considered whoring to be one of them."

He didn't want to, but I stood there for so long holding out the damn cheque that in the end I guess he had to. Wearing a pained expression, he headed for the door.

"You're being very silly about all this, you know, Chloe. We could have been good together, you know that. We're both on the up. The next Guy and Madge or Posh and Becks or whoever."

"I don't think so, Greg." I lay down on the bed, too exhausted to remove my clothes. I didn't even hear the door close.

chapter forty-one

I did try to get a plane home, but unless you had your own private jet – and I don't think even Buzz Longhi stretched to that – there was no chance, it being the height of the summer season, of changing your flight. Somehow I got through the time that remained, grateful that the size of the villa and its surroundings made it so easy to avoid bumping into someone you didn't want to see.

I slept late, and contrary to Rob's Australian wisdom, I took the sun at the worst possible time of the day – between twelve and three, when I could be guaranteed the pool to myself. So, I'd be a wizened prune by the time I was forty. Well, I'd hit that problem when I ran into it.

There was even room service, so I was spared having to sit in the same room as Greg to eat my meals. A couple of times I went back to that pizza place with Rob, but we never really recaptured the ease of that first meal. He seemed to be hanging back from me and I soon stopped searching him out. For one thing, it could have made things awkward for him if he'd been seen around with me too often and I couldn't blame him looking out for himself. I envied the cool way he made no secret of the fact he found the villa and the people there stultifying, disappearing whenever he could. I knew he was a keen photographer – a talent that wasn't at all surprising when you considered who his uncle was – and often he'd disappear for hours on end, presumably to take shots of the island in all its variety and beauty.

Occasionally I'd come across Tillie, who seemed to flit between members of Tough Love with such – to me – confusing regularity, that I began to wonder what her game was. Was she sleeping with all of them, I wondered, or were they all just really good chums? They certainly seemed to know how to have a high old time, both during the day and at night. High being the operative word.

She didn't seem to bear any malice towards me, considering I'd taken both her boyfriend and her prize job — and would smile at me sweetly whenever we ran across each other. One day she even invited me into her room to show me the dress she was going to wear for the party Buzz was throwing on the final evening. When I politely declined to share a few lines of coke with her she simply shrugged prettily and told me it was my loss and all the more for her.

"I'm not addicted to this stuff," she said, as she proceeded to clear a patch of her cluttered dressing table to make room for the operation she was about to perform. "I'm going to pack it all in — the booze, the pills, maybe hang on to the odd spliff for my nerves — but, honestly, as soon as we get home, that's it. Finito. But what the hell. I'm on holiday, aren't I? I'm not the only one here who's at it."

I found myself groping towards what I'd really been wanting to say since Greg had moved out of my room.

"I'm sorry Greg treated you so badly," I said. "You didn't deserve it."

"Please, Chloe. Don't mention him to me, ever. He's a part of my life I want to forget. I made a fool of myself. I don't need reminding."

"Is that why you take drugs? To blot it out?" I said.

"Chloe, look. I don't mean to be rude, but I'm not prepared to talk about any of that stuff with you. He's your boyfriend and I hope he treats you better, that's all. You won't get me to say anything more."

Already, a distant look was beginning to creep into her eyes. Tillie didn't even know that Greg and I were no longer together, although I guessed that most of her other pals had probably sussed it, even if Longhi and the press seemed none the wiser.

I knew better to talk to people about anything important when they were like this. Nothing they said made sense, and nothing you said made any difference to them, either. I changed the subject, and allowed Tillie to prattle on at length about the news she'd had from Kendall in Milan. When I slipped out of the room, I don't even think she noticed.

The day before we were due to go home was heavy with an oppressive heat that threatened storms later. I'd done my packing and even by lunchtime I was already wishing I was on the plane home. Mum and Dad and Lindsay would be travelling back from Northern France already, by my calculations, and would be home when I arrived.

By early evening it was raining heavily and any thoughts of holding the party outside on the terrace had been shelved.

"No worries," Tillie – who'd been behaving even more manically than usual since mid-afternoon – giggled. "We'll just have to trash the house instead. Just off to the little girls' room, so don't forget me when you pour the next round, Rob."

Emptying her glass to the dregs, she squinted as she searched for a flat surface to put it down on, then teetered off unsteadily. We were all – apart from Greg who was sulking in a corner with a bottle of water – drinking something Rob had mixed called "Catwalk Queen", a lethal cocktail whose recipe he'd gleaned from his bartender friend back in London.

When, fifteen minutes later, Tillie hadn't returned, I began to get anxious. I set off to find her. She could have been anywhere – although the weather forced me to discount outside. She wasn't in the nearest loo, nor was she to be found in any of the rooms on the ground floor. It was dark now, and a steady downpour drummed on the roof. Occasionally, a rumble of thunder thudded in the distance and a flash of lightning lit up the night.

"Tillie," I called out. My words echoed along the empty hallway.

With mounting apprehension I climbed the stairs and found myself approaching her room.

"Tillie," I called again, and rapped on the door. There was no answer. I rapped a third time. Nothing.

It was with a dry mouth and a sick feeling in my stomach that I let myself in. I'll never understand how I knew what I'd find, but when I saw Tillie sprawling face-down on the floor, her eyes open but somehow strangely devoid of light, a stream of spittle trailing from the side of her mouth and a thin brown liquid trickling from her nose, it wasn't fear or shock or surprise I felt, but the urgent need to get out of that room and get help.

It was no use shouting from here. No one would hear me above the music and laughter. Quick as I could, I hurtled downstairs and into the room where everyone was gathered.

"Get an ambulance!" I yelled. "It's Tillie. I think she's overdosed."

chapter forty-two

Things happened amazingly quickly after that. Someone turned the music off, people started shushing each other and an ambulance was summoned. Rob hurtled up the stairs and I hurtled after him, petrified that Tillie would be in a worse state than when I left her but too on edge to remain downstairs in ignorance.

I looked on while Rob put her in the recovery position, cursing myself for not thinking to do that before I left her alone to get help.

"Stay with her," he ordered. "I'm going to look for what she's taken. They'll need to know at the hospital – if they're going to be able to help her."

His words filled me with cold dread. Crouching

by her side, numb with fear, I stayed by her, stroking her forehead and squeezing her clammy hand until the ambulance arrived. All the time I spoke to her, doing my best to reassure her, but of course, it was as much Rob and myself I sought to reassure as Tillie.

"You're doing just great, Chloe," Rob said, as he meticulously searched every one of Tillie's drawers and cupboards in search of her stash.

"Got it," he breathed, just as the wail of the ambulance siren heralded its arrival. I didn't want to leave Tillie's side and protested when the medics showed up with Buzz Longhi in hot pursuit, but it quickly became apparent that with the arrival of Longhi, a transfer of control had taken place.

"We've been in touch with her mother," he snarled, as if the whole thing were just one more inconvenience on a par with the bad weather, "so you two might as well get packed up and ready to leave in the morning as planned."

Too exhausted to put up a fight, Rob and I did as he asked.

Next day, at the airport, he gave us all another pep talk. "If one word of this gets out, then you lot are finished," he said.

The band members – Greg included – cowered at Longhi's words and were still cowering as they unfastened their seat belts as the plane touched down at Heathrow.

As we scrambled for our hand luggage, Greg – who'd spent the whole of the journey sitting on his own, came over to me.

"What do you want?" I snapped. "Come to tell me again how sorry you are that Tillie nearly died last night?"

"Fuck off, Chloe. The silly cow had it coming. I'm surprised she's lasted this long. Messing up everybody's careers."

I've never thought of myself as a violent person but right then, if I'd had anything more dangerous on me than yesterday's rolled up newspaper – from which Kendall's stunning face peered out of the front page – I'd have clubbed him to death.

Greg must have seen Kendall's picture, because he said: "She's well out of it, that one. Perhaps I should have made more of a move on her instead of you."

"Do you ever think about anyone without considering how they can affect your career?" I snapped back.

Nothing he could say now could have any effect on me, I decided. But I was wrong.

"Just wait and see how quickly your agent drops you when this story breaks. Then you'll understand."

Greg's face was a mask of triumph. He hung around just long enough to see the horror at how this would look to Serena and my family, register on my face then he moved off.

Once we landed we were marshalled through to the VIP suite, then bundled towards a fleet of cars.

"Look, I just want to go home," I said to the suit in dark glasses who seemed to be policing the operation.

"Well, you'll have to wait, missy. This is a damage limitation exercise. Your party is being transferred to a safe house for a while."

When I protested and said my parents were expecting me home he told me it was for my own safety. I felt like I'd strayed into an episode of *The Sopranos*. When I tried to get support from my fellow travellers, all I got was meek looks.

I turned to Rob as a last resort, but all he said was, "Chloe, I don't think you've quite grasped the seriousness of this situation."

He spoke to me as if he were talking to a hysterical child. "For God's sake, Rob! Stop acting like a wimp," I yelled. "Why are you of all people going along with all this?"

Rob flinched at my words, and set his mouth in a grim line, but for some reason he didn't say a word in his own defence, which made me even madder.

"Do I care if Tough Love lose a few fans because they hang out with real people instead of the Teletubbies? Is this what all this is about? A way of protecting them from some bad publicity because one of their party has OD'd?"

"Partly," Rob conceded. "But the other thing, Chloe, is that once the shit hits the fan, you – as the person who found her – are going to be hounded night and day by the tabloid press. All this guy wants is to secure you some protection till they can contact your parents and Serena and decide how best to get you home in one piece."

I closed my eyes. This could not be happening to me. "Rob. I'm sorry I called you a wimp. But you've got to help me." I was beginning to think with the brain God gave me at last.

"Apology accepted," Rob said, very graciously considering, I thought. "But how can I?"

"Do you have transport? Can you drive me? I can't face Buzz Longhi right now, or Greg or any of them. I just want to get back home."

I think I was as near hysteria as I'd ever been. This was a nightmare and just as I thought I was leaving it behind, here it was again, shaking its ugly fist at me.

"Look, lady. I got my orders," the suit insisted. "You've got to get in the car alongside the rest of them. The both of you."

"Oh, yeah? You heard the lady? She wants to go home. If you try and stop her you'll have her lawyer to deal with." Rob reached inside his jacket pocket for his mobile phone and began to punch in someone's number furiously, while the suit looked on, horrified at the prospect of being threatened with a lawyer.

"You can tell Buzz Longhi to get lost," Rob said, mid-punch. "He doesn't employ me and he doesn't employ her, either. We'll make our own way home, if it's all the same to you."

I could have hugged Rob in gratitude.

The suit threw his hands up in the air, like it was absolutely nothing to do with him whatever we decided.

Finally, Rob got through to whoever was on the other end of the line. "Uncle Charlie? I need to borrow your car."

chapter forty-three

We were a couple of miles from home and my initial relief at getting away from Buzz Longhi's minder was beginning to turn into desperation. How was I going to face my parents after all this? When first Greg – with undisguised glee – then Rob, with anxious concern, had told me I'd be all over the papers once news about Tillie leaked out, I hadn't really taken either of them seriously.

I soon had plenty of cause to believe them, though. The first time was when Charlie McGrath eventually turned up with his car and with a grim face presented me with a bundle of newspapers. Pictures of Tillie plastered the front page accompanied by reports of her drug overdose. Pictures of me in Corsica, by the pool, on the beach – clearly taken with a long-lens camera because I'd had no idea at the time that anyone but me was there. Greg and me in happier times, arm in arm, gazing into each other's eyes. More recent pictures of both of us – sitting far apart, each looking in different directions. I thought about the fat photographer I'd always sneered at for being completely unaware that for most of the holiday Greg and I hadn't been together. Clearly, he wasn't as dumb as I'd imagined.

"Oh, fuck," was all I could say.

"Couldn't have put it better meself," Charlie McGrath said. "This is a bad business."

"It doesn't say anything bad about you though, Chloe. Says here that if you hadn't found her she would have been dead now," Rob interjected. "And she would you know, Charlie."

I was seconds away from bursting into tears.

"Here's the keys, Rob. Just get her home." To me Charlie said: "Listen, love. Tomorrow they'll be eating their fish and chips from these pages. By this time next week no one will even remember the story, let alone your part in it."

Charlie's kind words had started me off

snivelling like a snotty kid. Rob put his arm round me and handed me a tissue.

"Don't you be nice to me too," I sniffed, pushing him away.

He shrugged, like he was completely impervious to my feelings and said, "OK, buggerlugs. Just shut up and get in the car."

Don't ask me why but that made me feel much better. Until we hit the motorway and I realized that unless I got to a loo within the next ten minutes I would wet myself and Charlie McGrath's swish sports car into the bargain. When a reluctant Rob pulled into the next service station to let me out, then insisted on accompanying me as far as the door just in case, it hit home that the papers had already got hold of the story, or their twisted version of it, and people were already reading it.

Wearing my shades as some sort of disguise I managed to slip into the ladies' room and use the loo without anyone noticing me. But it was while I was washing my hands and face that I noticed two women through the mirror nudging and whispering.

"Isn't she that model who found that other one unconscious?" I heard the one say to the other.

"I could have sworn I've just seen her picture in my paper!"

There was more peering while her friend eyed me up and down. "Something about a drug-fuelled orgy, wasn't it?" she said. "Well, it certainly looks like her."

Silently I wished the hand-dryer would blow more powerfully so I could get out of there. When the plump woman's thin friend started to make her way over to me I was seized with fear. I cried out as she thrust something into my face, convinced she was going to hit me.

"Can I have your autograph?" she asked, waving what turned out to be a piece of paper.

I ran out with as much speed as I could summon, straight into Rob, grabbed his arm and raced with him to the car.

"The next hurdle's my mum and dad," I said, when I'd told him what had just happened. "Can you imagine it, Rob! They wanted my autograph! Just because I'd been in the paper!"

"They'll probably dine out on meeting you for weeks to come," Rob said, completely straight-faced. "They might even sell their story to the tabloids. MY WASH AND BRUSH UP WITH MODEL."

"Ha, ha, very funny. Now can we just get back in the car?"

The surrounding scenery was growing familiar. We'd be home in less than twenty minutes. Suddenly I remembered something else I'd overheard one of the women say, and my stomach gave a lurch while I wondered how on earth I was going to explain that one to my parents.

"Drug-fuelled orgy," I groaned. "Can you believe it?"

"Some people have all the luck," he said and smiled for the first time in ages.

"This is not funny, Rob," I said, but smiled too. Also for the first time in ages. "Listen," I went on. "You know, you've been really great, the way you stood up to that guy at the airport. Not to mention going to the trouble of driving me home. I can't thank you enough."

"I didn't have much choice, did I?" Rob said, without taking his eyes off the road. "And besides, I couldn't leave you in Greg's hands."

I groaned. "God, I've been such an idiot about him, haven't I? What on earth did I see in him?" Rob opened his mouth as if he were going to tell me, but I shut him up before he got going.

"You never liked him, did you?"

"That's very perceptive of you," Rob said.

"How much do you know about him, Rob?" It was suddenly important for me to know.

"I know he had a thing going with Tillie and when he dumped her she took it badly," he said. "And I know Kendall was in such a rage about it that she said killing him would be worth serving life imprisonment for."

Oh, God. Kendall. All those awful things I'd thought and said about her, some of them to Rob. The worst thing was that I'd believed Greg's version of events over hers.

"I asked her more than once what had really happened between Greg and Tillie, because whatever it was seemed to upset Tillie more than any other of her broken romances, but she said Tillie had insisted she keep quiet about what had really happened, so I didn't push it. You don't with Kendall."

"No, I think I gathered that pretty early on," I said.

"Don't be so down on her, Chloe. Apart from all her family problems, Kendall's a loyal friend. Not everybody would have stood by Tillie like she has.

And it's not everyone who can keep a secret, either. I can't imagine she'd ever give away what really happened to Tillie, unless it was for a good reason."

I swallowed hard. Kendall had had a good reason to tell me Tillie's real story, all right. She'd wanted to warn me off Greg. She'd been trying to help me all along, and I'd snubbed her. I fell into a brooding silence about the mess I'd got into.

"Oh, by the way." Rob's words startled me out of it. "Hope you don't mind, but I took the liberty of buying your sister a little prezzie on the plane. Part of her therapy."

In all this I hadn't given Lindsay a single thought! And the very last thing I'd said to her before I left for Corsica was that I'd bring her back a souvenir!

"Rob. God, what a selfish bitch I am. There's poor Tillie in hospital and poor Lindsay struggling to get better at home and all I can do is think about myself. How can I thank you?"

"Well, you can give me the money."

"Sure." I scrabbled in my bag, glad to be able to do something practical to take my mind off the fact that in less than two minutes Rob would be turning off the main road into my street — which was more of a cul-de-sac, actually, with my house right at the bottom — and I would be facing the music. "How much do I owe you?"

"Thirty quid. It's a watch. Really neat one, actually."

"Bloody hell, Rob, that's very generous of you."

"SHIT!"

"You'll have to wait till we get in and I can write you a — JESUS CHRIST! You can't drive down there. We'll be lynched!"

But it was too late. The mob of reporters and photographers — from where I was sitting it looked like at least twenty — had spotted the car and were heading our way.

"What do I do?" Rob had started to sweat. "Chloe, what do you want me to do?"

"I don't know. Christ, I don't know! What does Robbie Williams do when he gets mobbed?"

"Grab my mobile. Ring the police."

But before I could locate the mobile in the glove compartment, we heard the sound of sirens, two police cars came screeching round the corner and six burly police officers leaped out as their cars squealed to a halt.

Rob let out a long low whistle of amazement. "So that's what you pay taxes for," he said, as one of the police officers headed towards us.

chapter forty-four

I have never been so relieved to see my parents. Come to think of it, I'd never seen them so relieved to see me since the day I left home after a row when I was seven and hid in the shed until it started to get dark.

Mum bustled in with a tray full of tea things and Lindsay, wearing her new wristwatch with pride and looking so much better than when I'd last seen her, followed behind carrying another one laden with scones, a pot of jam and butter.

"You saved that poor girl from certain death by the sounds of things," Mum said proudly.

"I only did what anybody would have done, Mum," I said, embarrassed. "I had a feeling, that was all, and I acted on it. Rob did much more than I did."

"Boy Scout stuff, that's all," Rob said modestly, looking up from his plate.

"Well, whatever it was, it worked. And we can't thank you enough for taking such care of Chloe, either."

"Oh, that one can take care of herself," he said darkly.

Mum clearly appreciated Rob's insight into my personality, but I didn't. Instead I stuck my tongue out at him and he did the same back. He turned his attention back to Lindsay and said, "Can I put a bit of butter and jam on one of these for you, Lindsay – while I'm doing one for me, I mean?"

Lindsay visibly preened at the attention and accepted graciously. Mum and I looked on indulgently, while she chattered on, Rob occasionally interrupting with a question.

"He knows about Lindsay," I whispered.

She looked over to the two of them again and nodded with satisfaction.

"Is he your new boyfriend?" she whispered back.

I felt myself blushing furiously. "He's just a friend!" I hissed.

"Well, stop flirting with him then. Can't you see he fancies you?" Mum hissed.

Was I flirting? I looked up again at Rob, who was waving a scone around and laughing at some joke of Lindsay's. It seemed strange to see him in our poky living room after the gracious house we'd shared in Corsica. But he seemed to fit here much more comfortably than he'd ever done in those surroundings. So much so that it was getting dark before he left. The friendly Mr Plod on our doorstep stood to one side to let him out.

"We'll go and visit Tillie as soon as she's allowed to fly back," he promised. "She'll need some cheering up."

"Sure."

"I can look the other way if you want me to," the policeman interjected.

Rob and I exchanged embarrassed glances at the man's misunderstanding of the situation and in the same moment I said that Rob wasn't my boyfriend, he said that I wasn't his girlfriend.

It was a relief when Lindsay broke the cringe-making silence with her yell of: "Phone for you, Chloe."

"Oh. OK," I called back. "Thanks, Rob. You've been great."

"Go and answer the phone, Chloe," Rob said. "I'll speak to you soon."

Then he was gone, leaving me feeling like I'd missed saying something important.

"Right, I'm knocking off now," the policeman said. "Looks like your fifteen minutes of glory's come to an end already. There's not a hack in sight."

But when I picked up the phone, it was clear that it hadn't even started.

"Chloe Dove?"

Was this a reporter? I wondered.

"This is Chloe Dove. Who am I speaking to?"

"YOU BITCH!"

I held the phone away from my ear, reeling from the insult.

"You've no idea who I am, have you? But I know you. I've seen your face plastered all over the newspapers with him."

Clearly, this was some deranged fan of Greg's. But how had she got my number?

"Who the hell are you?" I yelled at the receiver.

"My name's Charmaine King. Ring any bells?"

"Should it?"

A beat and then: "So Greg's never even mentioned my name to you?"

I was beginning to feel uneasy. "Greg?" I croaked.

"My fiancé. The boy I fell in love with when we were both fourteen. Childhood sweethearts, we were. Never apart until the day he left for the big city to seek fame and fortune. Left with my encouragement — not to mention £500 of my savings. He was off like a shot, never mind his responsibilities."

Some men are bigamists. Greg was turning out to be a serial fiancé.

"Look, Charmaine, you'd better know that Greg and me are finished. If he owes you money you should be talking to him, not me."

"Do you think I haven't tried?" The girl seemed to have stopped being furious now and sounded weary instead. It was this resignation in her voice that convinced me that she wasn't making her story up.

"When he left we wrote and phoned for six months or so. Then the letters and the phone calls just dried up. I've written to his record company but all I've had is a signed photograph. As if that will pay the heating bills," she added bitterly.

"Charmaine," I said, as gently as I could. "Greg's moved on. Perhaps you should just let him go. After all, you have no claims on him."

"Have I not?" The anger was rising in her voice again. "Have you any idea what it feels like to see pictures of him living the high life with models and millionaires and people who can shove fifty quid's worth of coke up their noses in less time it takes me to earn two quid?"

"What do you want me to do? I said we were finished. As far as I'm concerned I couldn't care less if I see Greg again. I've even deleted his phone number, so if you want to get in touch with him you'll have to find some other way."

"Don't worry. I already have. I'm going to the press. Let's see what his fans think when they learn how he walked out on me three months before his baby girl was born."

chapter forty-five

It was the next morning and I was still in bed, too depressed to drag myself downstairs to face the world. I peeped through my curtains, certain that outside things had hotted up again. I was right. The reporters were back, some smoking, some drinking coffee from flasks while they eyed the house and exchanged jokes and comments with each other. What was this? A party?

Dad came into my room without knocking and threw the papers on my bed. He looked grey and drawn. "Have a look at these. It's pretty shitty. Serena's phoned and she's on her way."

After just one quick glance at the front page I groaned and fell back on my pillow. "She'll sack me for sure. Greg was right. Is she livid?"

"No," Dad said. "Why should she be? All she said was that you're well out of it and she was driving over to discuss tactics. Meanwhile, say nothing to anyone and don't even think about showing yourself to that pack of wolves outside." When he gave the curtains a twitch a dozen cameras clicked and flashed. "Now, are you going to read this?"

Today there was a new headline. Tillie's story had been relegated to page four, where I learned that close friends had said she'd been booked into an exclusive rehab centre. Well, if Serena was on her way then I could soon check the veracity of that report.

Emblazoned on the front page was the headline: THEY'RE THE ONES – POP STAR TURNS BACK ON FAMILY FOR FAME.

It was all there in black and white – every sordid detail of Greg's life before he reinvented himself as Mr Smooth.

"Twenty-year-old Charmaine says: 'Greg would be nowhere without me. I believed in him, I even gave him all my money. He was going to go to London and make it big and then send for Billie and me. Well, he did the first two things, but he somehow forgot the last. Now it's his turn to put his hand in his pocket.'"

The photograph on the front page showed Charmaine, dark-haired, plump and pretty, with a little girl in her arms who was Greg's double. Inside were two more pages of photographs and speculation. Here was the picture shown yesterday of Greg and me gazing lustfully into each other's eyes with the caption: "Champagne lifestyle for Greg and glamorous girlfriend Chloe Dove while Charmaine 'buys Billie's clothes at jumble sales'."

A more recent picture showed Greg looking surly — clearly he'd been snapped yesterday when we'd gone our separate ways. "No comment" was the caption beneath that particular photograph. There was some pretty nasty stuff about his "callous" behaviour, alongside quotes from fans who swore they'd never buy another of Tough Love's records. I wondered how many reporters would be hanging around outside his home right now. What would Buzz Longhi be doing for "damage limitation" this time?

I felt almost gleeful until Dad said, "Chloe. I'm warning you before you turn the page. I'm afraid there's something else."

But it was too late, I already had. There I was, arm in arm with Kelly, clearly drunk and giving the finger to whoever was taking the snap. It was a picture of the two of us at somebody's birthday party last year, when Kelly and I had been best buddies, before I'd even heard of Greg Geffen and the idea of me being spotted by a model scout would have been laughed off the face of the planet by anyone who knew me. I remembered it was some would-be boyfriend of Kelly's who'd taken that photo. He'd got this new digital camera and I was getting pretty fed up because he'd already taken about six shots of her when I was trying to have a conversation with her. Hence the finger.

"MODEL CHLOE TOO BIG FOR HER BOOTS" was the headline on this page. I read on, tripping over the words in my eagerness. What followed was a tirade by Kelly – who was described not very originally as "a bubbly blonde wannabe actress". Apparently – according to this report – once I'd been snapped up by "top model agency Olympus", I'd dropped all my friends.

"Chloe and I shared everything, but the night she ignored me for Tough Love's Greg Geffen was the night I knew that fame had finally gone to her head."

I was distracted from the page by a commotion outside. Serena's car had pulled up and the reporters were falling over each other in an attempt to get a quote from her. I watched from my window as she marched up to our front door, completely stonewalling them. Then some unseen member of the family managed to let her in while at the same time keeping everyone else out.

Reaching for my dressing gown I reluctantly trailed downstairs. From Serena's grim face I was in for a roasting, whatever she'd told Dad on the phone. I preferred to get it out of the way sooner rather than later. Mum and Dad were perched on the edge of the couch. I noticed the curtains were closed even though it was daylight outside.

"Oh," she said caustically, as I popped my head round the door. "So you can spare the time in your increasingly tabloid existence to come and talk to your agent, then."

I held up my hands in self-defence. "Serena. I swear. I have never taken drugs in my life. I knew nothing about this Charmaine girl until last night and whatever Kelly has to say is a complete fib. You've got to believe me."

"Of course I do," Serena said, impatiently. "But

346

one thing I can blame you for – going out with that Greg Geffen! Pop stars are always bad news, in my experience. Why couldn't you have chosen some-one a bit more reliable? A double axe-murderer for instance?"

Mum and Dad snorted at Serena's joke, which I thought was in very poor taste, actually.

"Anyway, I'm not here to discuss your love life. I'm here to offer you some work and to plan how we're going to deal with this – er, unfortunate state of affairs."

"Work? Modelling work?" I flopped down into the nearest chair. "Honestly, Serena. I've had it with modelling. It's brought me nothing but trouble. I want you to take me off your books – from today."

"Nonsense." Serena swatted my opposition away with one wave of her imperious hand. "You have the makings of a very good model. You're in-telligent, you catch on quickly, and more importantly you don't take yourself too seriously."

Flattery would get her nowhere. "I mean it. The next time I have my picture taken will be for my NUS card," I said.

"Chloe. You've had a spot of bad publicity.

Obviously, you're a bit upset. But you've got to get through this like the winner I know you to be. Now, have you heard of Acharavi cosmetics?"

I shook my head wearily.

"Ooh, I remember that brand. It was all the rage when I was a girl," Mum said. "I still see it around in the shops, only it seems a bit dated nowadays."

"Exactly," Serena said, addressing Mum. "Staid. Safe. But they're planning a relaunch and they want Chloe here to be their face. They were keen on her before, but after all this – well, they rather think some of your notoriety will rub off on their name and people will think it's cool to wear Acharavi once more."

When she told me how much they were prepared to pay I was staggered, but still unmoved. No amount of money would make me change my mind.

"I won't do it," I said flatly.

Serena raised one eyebrow. "Well, I suppose I could try to get them to up the offer a little bit, but we can't get too ambitious."

"No. I'm not interested in money. I'm not interested in modelling. I told you, I quit."

Serena blinked and looked at Mum and Dad for

support. She wasn't getting any from Dad.

"Chloe's old enough to make her own mind up about what she wants to do," he said, which flew in the face of everything he'd ever said to me for the past eighteen years.

"You're upset just at the moment, Chloe. I can see you might not want to get involved in this campaign, but surely there'd be no harm in a bit of catalogue work." Even Mum was trying to cajole me, now! What had happened to female solidarity?

Serena threw up her hands in horror. "Catalogue work! With great respect, Mrs Dove, I don't think Chloe will be doing catalogue work ever again. Not if I have anything to do with it. This girl is dynamite right now. There might even be an acting career in it."

I thought of Kelly, and how she'd probably have given her eye teeth to be where I was now. But I was no actor and I'd never been a seeker of fame.

In words of one syllable, I told Serena so.

"Chloe, listen, sweetheart," she said. "Maybe you're right. Maybe the Acharavi campaign isn't for you. After all, we don't want people starting to think of you as that girl in the drugs and baby story. In the long term it won't look good."

She seemed to be doing some calculations in her head. Then she said, "Now, I want you to stop worrying. What I'm going to do is give you the keys to my little retreat by the sea in Wales. I want you to go down there for a week or so, have a nice rest and when you come back all this —" she waved her hand in the direction of the window where the news hounds were still baying for my blood — "will be a distant memory."

She turned to Mum and Dad. "I wouldn't do this for many of my girls, Mr and Mrs Dove, but Chloe's different. She's special. I don't quite know what it is but she has a quality about her that I predict will give her a lot of work in the years ahead. Some of my girls would be happy to have their faces plastered all over the papers — not to mention other bits of their anatomy — but not Chloe. She knows her own worth. Not like poor Tillie."

"How is Tillie?" I wanted to know.

"She'll be in hospital a week. Here's the address and her private number. Oh, and a note from Rob. About going to visit her, I guess."

I took the bit of paper from her, barely glancing at its contents.

"Now, Chloe," Serena said, clapping her hands together like she'd just made some major decision. "You might not like what I'm going to ask you to do now. But I really think that if you give just one interview to one paper, then they'll leave you alone."

I was aghast. Was anyone going to leave me alone ever again?

"Do you think that's wise?" Dad butted in. "How do we know what angle they're going to take?"

"We'll make it an exclusive," Serena said. "We'll give the money to Charmaine so no one can accuse Chloe of benefiting financially."

I could see from the glint in Dad's eye that he was coming round to the idea.

"Course, it will make Greg look like a complete cad, which will be no bad thing," she added, a smile of satisfaction creeping over her face.

chapter forty-six

Serena was right. As soon as I did the interview and it appeared in one newspaper, the press melted away. It came out on the same day as Greg's own remorseful account of his treatment of Charmaine and his neglect of his daughter Billie.

"MY SHAME WILL NEVER LEAVE ME" went the headlines. A touching account of how Greg had learned his bad parenting skills from his own neglectful father followed. My heart bled for him.

Serena rang me the day the two stories appeared almost side by side.

"The nerve of the boy! It'll be that Buzz Longhi's put him up to this. A pack of lies from start to finish. Just wait till tomorrow. I bet you any money there'll be a follow-on about how he's rediscovered fatherhood. There'll be wall-to-wall pictures of him bouncing this poor wretched Billie on his knee and looking hunky at the same time. The fans will lap it up. Now have you thought any more about moving to London? That's where all the work is, you know."

I sighed. What was it about Serena that made her only hear what she wanted to? I reminded her of our conversation the previous day.

"Nothing's happened to change my mind," I said.

"Oh? Well, maybe this will. How do you fancy going on safari in Africa?"

I gulped.

"I don't know the details yet, but if you want to try for it, then I'll do everything I can to get you the job."

Serena was like a cat with a bird. She just wouldn't give up. "Look, Serena. I really can't think about this stuff," I sighed. "Talk to me when I get back from Wales."

"Well, of course, darling! Never let it be said that I pressurize people! That's never been my style."

Yeah, right.

It was nothing more than the truth when I told Serena how much I was looking forward to Wales. I was taking Lindsay, who, since my return from Corsica, had taken to following me about with puppy-like devotion. She made me feel like a real louse. All those awful names I'd called her in the past. Compared to Kendall, I'd not been much of a sister. Well, maybe I could make amends, starting with this holiday. And who knew, perhaps she'd stop being so uncharacteristically nice to me once we got there and she got over her misplaced gratitude.

When Kendall called the next day I nearly dropped the phone. She wanted to thank me for what I'd done for Tillie, she said. She'd heard the whole story from Rob, who'd kept in touch through everything while she'd been away in Italy. I bet he had, I thought, grimly.

"I saw the card and the daft teddy and flowers you sent her too. They really cheered her up."

"Honestly, it's nothing," I insisted. "I really want to go and see her. I'm off to Wales soon with my sister. But getting to the hospital isn't that easy without transport. Everything's in London, isn't it?"

Everything and everyone, I couldn't help thinking. I imagined Rob and Kendall sitting on Tillie's bed, eating her chocolates and popping her grapes into each other's mouths. I blinked away the image and at the same time it flashed through my head that I was exhibiting the classic symptoms of jealousy.

Before I could think about this more deeply, Kendall said, "Serena told me you'd said you were thinking of packing in modelling?"

My, how news travelled! "Not thinking about it. Have done."

"So, what will you do instead?"

I shrugged. For the first time I realized I hadn't given this particular topic any thought at all.

"Chloe? You still there?"

"Yeah."

"They say shelf-stacking at Sainsbury's pays well."

"Look, has Serena put you up to this?"

"This what?"

"This. . ." I struggled to find the right word. "This bullying."

"No!" But Kendall was clearly laughing. "Listen. I won't mention it again. Well, not for a bit, anyway. But are you serious about visiting Tillie?"

"Sure. But like I said. How do I get there?"

"Easy-peasy. I'll come and get you."

I tried all the objections I could. The distance, the cost of petrol, the inconvenience to Kendall, but she would have none of it. Within an hour she was outside the door, elegant and ultra-cool, even in her faded jeans and T-shirt.

"We'll go right away, if you don't mind," she said, as I got in. "Only I've got something on later and I'll have to dash if I'm going to get back to the flat and changed in time."

"But. . ."

Hadn't she forgotten that she'd promised to drive me back? There was no way I could visit Tillie if I was going to be stranded at some hospital miles from anywhere without the transport home.

"Don't worry about the return journey," she reassured me, although I was far from reassured. "Rob'll bring you. He's quite familiar with the route, or so he tells me."

"I can't ask him to bring me home again," I wailed. "Besides, won't he be going with you to wherever it is you're going to?"

"No. Why would he?" We were in the car by this

time, already heading out of town.

"Well, I thought. You and Rob . . . you know."

Kendall threw back her head and roared, narrowly missing knocking a cyclist off his bike.

"Honestly, some people would be better off on public transport," she said. "Rob's a mate, that's all. He helps me with my mum, sometimes. Looks in on her when I can't, that sort of thing."

Somewhere deep inside I felt the slow unfurling of promise. It was hard to keep my mind on what I knew I had to say next, which was just as important as these other feelings stirring inside.

"Rob told me about your family situation. It must be difficult for you."

Kendall shrugged in acknowledgement. "Used to it," she said. "Mum's been ill all my life. My brother and I do what we can. I do the modelling to pay for all the stuff she has to have. Dad buggered off at the first sign, so we had no choice."

"Men, eh? Look, Kendall. I'm sorry I ever doubted you." There, now I'd said it. "About Greg, I mean."

"You had to get him out of your system. Think of him like a bad fashion mistake."

We grinned at each other.

"You know he's gone back to that Charmaine, don't you?"

I didn't. After my brush with the tabloid press, I'd vowed never to buy another newspaper again.

"She must be crackers wanting that one back. He'll destroy her if she'll let him."

"He didn't destroy me," I reminded her. "*Au contraire*, actually."

"Well, let's hope she's got your bollocks."

We were driving through the gates of an imposing Victorian hospital now. Kendall whipped out a disabled sticker and slapped it on the windscreen. "This should see us right for the next hour or so," she said. "Don't look so appalled, Chloe, I am legitimately entitled to this badge, you know. Now, follow me. I know this place like the back of my hand."

When we finally reached Tillie's private room, after we'd walked down a labyrinth of corridors, the first person I saw was Rob. He was poking around in Tillie's bedside cupboard, on his haunches, his back to the door.

"Nice butt," Kendall mouthed at me, and winked.

She wasn't wrong. I tried to fasten my gaze elsewhere, but spectacularly failed to.

"You'll have to be a bit more specific about where you think this nail polish is you know, Tillie," he was saying, then quickly spun round as Tillie whooped with glee at seeing us.

"Steady, girl." Kendall gave me a playful dig in the ribs. She'd noticed the way I looked at Rob, completely overjoyed to see him. Was it my imagination, or was he equally pleased to see me? Tillie certainly was.

She looked very thin and very pale – even more waif-like than usual. But there was nothing waif-like about her manner. On the contrary, she seemed shot through with a steely determination. She was going into rehab and then she would be moving to Paris, where her mother lived. She intended starting her life again.

"I'll get over this, you know," she said. "I promise you."

"You betcha," Rob said, and squeezed her hand.

"I've already arranged to have my trunk sent over to France," she said. "So, whenever you're ready you can move your stuff in, Chloe."

"What?" I said, dumbstruck.

"You moving to London?" Rob said, at the same time.

"Kendall, you haven't even asked her!" Tillie wailed.

"OK, I'm sorry," Kendall said. "We got talking about other stuff and I didn't get round to it." She turned to me with pleading eyes. "Listen, Chloe," she said. "Please, please give up any stupid idea you might have about giving up modelling. Try it for a year. There's even a room waiting for you in the flat."

"Giving up modelling! Why on earth would you want to do that?" Rob and Tillie exclaimed simultaneously.

Kendall grinned at me like I hadn't a leg to stand on. Clearly, I hadn't.

"Well," I said. "Maybe I could give it a try. Just for a few months, that is. I suppose the money's got to be better than the minimum wage. And a flat in London. . ."

"Good girl," Kendall said. "Look, you've managed to cheer Rob up! Hasn't she, Rob?" She was clearly teasing him, and enjoying it.

Rob glared at her.

"What's got into you today, Rob?" she went on. "You've been in a bit of a state ever since we got here."

"I'm not in a bit of a state," he growled.

"Aw, come on. You can't seem to stay in one place for a minute at a time. Got something on your mind?"

"No, I haven't!"

Kendall gave him a gleeful grin, clearly delighted she'd succeeded in embarrassing him even further. "Take a chill pill!" she said.

We chatted for a while longer, then Kendall caught sight of the time. "Bloody hell. Listen Tillie, my darling, I've got to go. I've got this hot date tonight and it's gonna take me hours to get ready."

There followed a frantic round of farewell kisses, then Kendall's hand flew to her mouth like she'd just remembered something.

"Rob. Poor Chloe's stuck unless you can drive her home. You won't let her down, will you?"

Well, what choice did he have?

"So," he said, once we were on our own.

It wasn't my imagination. The sticky awkwardness between us was coming just as much from him as from me. Why didn't I just tell him I really fancied him? Because I sure as hell did, and I wasn't sure how much longer I could keep on pretending I just wanted him as a friend. Was it mutual?

Everyone but me seemed to think it was. My mum, that stupid policeman on our step who said that he would look away while we said goodnight, even Kendall.

"You're moving to London, then?" I'd have expected something better from Rob. Not that I could do much better myself.

"Yes. Well, I'll have to give it more thought. But, well, you never know."

Silence, then, "But I'm going to Wales first. With my sister."

"Your sister. How is she?"

"She's great. Got her old beans back."

"Beans?"

"Nothing. I mean, she's full of beans."

This went on for ages. Still awkward, not companionable. I fiddled with the radio and got Tough Love. Be The One. I switched it off, hurriedly, but not before Rob caught my eye. He winked. Like you would to a mate. My stomach contracted.

"You were great with Tillie," he said. "Really sweet."

Was he saying he fancied me? Why couldn't he be more obvious?

"I like her, that's all. It's easy to be nice to people when you like them."

"I guess."

Still nothing. I ploughed on.

"So. What are your plans, Rob? After the summer."

"Well, my gap year's nearly over. Is truly over, I guess."

My heart sank. Why hadn't it occurred to me that Rob would be going back to Australia once the summer was finished?

"I've got a place at uni to do photography."

"That's nice." I was lying.

"Do you mind if we just pull over into this service station? I think I need a pee."

"Be my guest." I thought I was going to cry. I stared at his big hands on the wheel as he manoeuvred the car to a standstill under a shady tree.

"So where's the course? Sydney? Melbourne? The University of Wogga-Wogga?"

"I thought we'd declared an amnesty on the Aussie jokes?"

"Sorry."

More silence.

"So where, then? Are you ever going to get round to telling me?"

I was in despair.

"London, actually." He grinned at me.

"You bastard," I squealed. "You absolute bastard!"

I leaned forward to pummel his chest for teasing me for so long. Rob raised his arms in mock surrender, and then they were around my shoulders and I found myself sliding into his embrace.